SHADOW CASTER

THE NIGHTWATCH ACADEMY BOOK 1

DEBBIE CASSIDY

CONTENTS

ONE

THEN

"Indie! Indie! Indie!" The crowd was going wild.

Blood, sweat, and more blood speckled the sawdust. Probably a few teeth too. Not mine, though, because that was the sound of *my* name they were screaming.

Mine.

This fight was mine.

The moonkissed, hairy bastard glared at me through his remaining eye. I'd gouged out the other one. No biggie. It would grow back. And now he bared his fangs and charged.

I held my ground, boots planted firmly in the dust. One. Two. Three. I leapt, scaling his frame easily to land behind him. He hit the barbed fence, howled, and spun to face me just in time to receive an epic uppercut.

His eyes rolled back in his head, and he went down.

"Whooo!"

The pit was filled with a deafening roar. Time to take my signature curtsy—pouted lips and fluttering lashes.

The crowd whooped in appreciation of the petite nightblood with the delicate features who kicked ass like a prime-alpha. Not that any prime-alphas had been seen or heard of for a long while. Still, their fighting prowess was legendary.

And so was mine.

Leaving the moonkissed unconscious in the dust, I strode out of the pit.

Ned greeted me at the gates. "You did good, kid." He hopped from foot to foot.

He was a good-looking creature with a golden mop of hair he liked to hide beneath a stylish flat cap. His leprechaun blood made him small in stature, but the ladies who'd been invited into his bedroom loved to discuss how he made up for any shortcomings in height with impressive expansions in other areas of his anatomy.

And me? He'd shoved me straight in the off-limits zone when he'd started calling me kid. Maybe I just wasn't the horny fey-blood's type.

Shame.

"And look at ya." He raked me up and down. "Not even a scratch on ya."

I grinned down at him. "I healed faster than he could injure, is all. And look, the crowd's nice and warmed up for you."

"You ever going to let me pay ya?" He canted his head, one eye closed in a wince-wink.

It was his come-on-give-in-to-me look, but it didn't work on me.

I tapped the lip of his cap. "Letting me in that pit is payment enough."

Besides, if I took his money, I'd never burn through daddy's little trust fund. No matter how much I spent, it kept getting topped up. I'd tried cutting myself off, going dark, and living off the tips I made working at Ned's bar, but my father always found me.

Power gave Baron Justice eyes and ears everywhere. Well, let him hear about this—his only child hanging with the dregs of supernatural society. A high-born nightblood slumming it with the rabble in an area of London we liked to call Dark Market, a large area filled with supernatural dives mostly tucked away from human eyes.

Ha. Take that, Daddy Dearest.

I turned my head and spat out the blood gathering in my mouth. It was all very well when the blood was someone else's but not so yummy when it was my own.

Ned's dark eyes gleamed. "Got a pressie for you in your cubicle." He winked. "Hope you like it."

My stomach grumbled. "You, my man, are a legend."

I wove through the crowd, the cheer of the pit rising behind me as a new fight began. Body odors mingled, sweet and sour, heartbeats competed in tempo, and I allowed my senses to open and enjoy the cocktail of smells and sounds pressing in on me. They grounded me. The regulars knew better than to accost me after a fight. Trying to hit pause on a hungry nightblood was asking to be bitten.

Hard.

Our world was a lie, an illusion. The fanged and the hairy, the feyblood, and all types of scary hid in the shadows. We allowed the universal glamour that existed on the mortal plane to mute the effect of our unhuman irises and smooth out our fangs. We allowed it to hide our horns and scales so we could look human to the human eye. The Nightwatch claimed we were protecting the humans, but the truth was we were protecting ourselves.

It was all about saving our own asses, because if the humans wanted, they could kill the fuck out of us. Okay, not the most eloquent way to put it. But still. It was the truth. We had magic—weavers who could manipulate threads of arcana in the air, and make shit happen. But if it ever came to an *us* and *them*, the humans had the weapons, the science, and the numbers to bring us down.

So, we played by the rules. We scuttled and hid

during the day. Blended in where possible. But the night ... The night was ours, and places like Ned's Pit were dens of inequity where the supernaturals got to let their hair down and play. Didn't mean the odd human didn't sneak in. They were drawn to places like that, explaining away what they saw, blaming it on drugs and booze and fetishes. In a place like that, I didn't need to use suggestion to get what I wanted. It was handed to me.

Blood.

My gums ached, my stomach rumbled, and then my cubicle came into view. The top of a tousled dark head peeked over the back of the seat. I inhaled, tasting him with my senses.

Male, young, probably early twenties.

Nice.

And then a hand wrapped itself around my bicep. "Indigo Justice, we need to talk."

I looked slowly from the pale fingers gripping my olive skin up to the death-wish dude's face, my expression flat. This was his cue to let go, but the douche seemed to be insensitive to the nuances of the very simple situation.

I guess I'd have to spell it out for him. "If you plan on keeping that hand, I suggest you remove it from my arm."

He sighed and released me. "Miss Justice, I've been sent to retrieve you."

I blinked at him in surprise. It had been almost six

months since my father had tried this shit. I'd sent his men back bloody and bruised, and he'd left me alone ever since. I guess my grace period was up.

I puffed out my cheeks, not in the mood for another fight, especially not on an empty stomach. "Listen ..."

"Earl."

"Yeah, listen, Earl. I don't want to hurt you."

He smiled, showcasing his lethal fangs. "I don't wish to hurt you either."

"Oh, goody. Then we have an understanding. You can tell my father you tried to bring me back. Say I kicked you in the head and knocked you out. He'll understand."

Earl locked gazes with me. "You won't leave here without a fight, will you?"

I clenched my jaw, biting back my irritation. "I won't be leaving, period."

He had one minute, and then I'd forget how hungry I was and stomp on his face. One minute to make the smart choice and fuck off.

He nodded. "Very well. It was a pleasure meeting you." He took a step back, turned, and melted into the crowd.

I guess my reputation had preceded me. My gut twinged in a warning my stomach wouldn't let me focus on. Food first, mental shit later. My snack awaited, and he was peering over the top of the seat, his warm brown eyes searching the crowd for me. I raised a hand as I approached. He shuffled along the seat to allow me to join him.

Slender, wiry, wide-eyed. Mmmm. "Hi, my name's Indigo."

His throat bobbed. "I know who you are." His smile was shaky, nervous. "I've never been ... bitten before."

Ooh, a bite virgin. Ned, you dark horse. I stroked his arm. "Oh, you don't have to be afraid. I promise this won't hurt. In fact, you're going to love it."

He took a deep breath, exhaled, and then tipped his head to the side to expose his throat. His pulse beat fast, which meant the blood would flow faster. This would be a real hit to my system.

I sidled up to him, my body brushing his. God, he smelled good. Fresh like cotton and summer nights. My fangs elongated, sliding out from my gums with a snick, and then my mouth was sucking on his flesh, creating a seal. Perfect. He tensed, anticipating the penetration.

I stroked his chest to soothe him. There, there, pet. And then I sank my teeth into him. Sweet, coppery flavor rushed into my mouth. Yes. God, yes, I needed that. Still warm from the vein, it flowed down my throat and hit my stomach. I hadn't realized how famished I was until that moment, until human blood was in my mouth. My gulps were too loud as I devoured my meal.

I needed to stop in a moment, but the hunger, which should have eased, flared hot and potent in my belly, and a red haze entered my mind. My taste buds registered the slight bitter undertone to the blood flooding my mouth and panic flared in my chest.

Something was wrong. The blood was tainted. This wasn't right. But I couldn't stop.

Fight, dammit. Fight and—

My primal brain took over, and then there was nothing but crimson glory.

THE CUFFS on my wrist reflected my angry face. I'd been cocky, distracted. Hungry. I should have known when Earl backed off so easily that something was wrong. I should have stopped and listened to my gut.

Too late now.

The room was small. Six by six, with a bolted-down table and two Formica chairs—one either side.

Idiots, a chair was probably a better weapon than a table. Should have bolted that down too, not that it would do me any good, not while the cuffs were cutting into my flesh. I knew what these were—electrocharged restraints used on prisoners.

Prisoner.

Me.

Murderer.

Me.

My stomach rolled with nausea. I'd killed the human. I'd drained him, and now the powers that be had me. Locked in a pretty cell with a fake mirror while they decided what my fate should be.

This was all him, and this was his power.

Fuck this shit. I was done waiting. I stood and approached the two-way mirror. "I know you're there, *Dad*. Stop fucking about, and let's get this over with."

Less than a minute passed before the door opened and my father strode in. Dressed to impress as usual—some tailored shit for a suit, hair slicked back, slate gray eyes flat and unemotional as he stared down at me.

"You killed a human, Indigo. That's a crime punishable by death or lifetime incarceration."

"You put something in his blood. You drugged him. *You* did this."

He sighed. "Interesting accusations. You believe your loss of control was due to a substance in your victim's blood?" He tapped his chin, mouth turning down slightly. "It is a possibility, but unfortunately, since the human body has been incinerated, pursuant to Watch Code 301, there is no way to test your theory."

My insides tightened in panic. There was no doubt in my mind that my father was responsible for my being here. Earl had planted that mark. He'd offered me the chance to leave with him, and I'd turned him down. The human had been their plan B.

Arguing with him was pointless, though. He had me here, where he wanted me. Question was, why? "What do you want?"

"I want to save my only child."

My throat pinched. Damn, why did my fucking heart pulse harder at those words? Why the hell did I still want to believe him?

I grit my teeth. "Since when have you given a damn about me? You care about your reputation and your name. You've got no need for a daughter. You've made that abundantly clear over the years."

He stood tall, looking down his nose at me. "Regardless, you are a Justice. And you belong with us. I've spoken to the council, and they've agreed to a deal. They'll waive a trial and sentencing in lieu of you pledging yourself to the Nightwatch."

My ears buzzed with the implication of his words. "You want me to ... to join the fucking Watch?"

"I want you to enroll at the Academy. I want you to graduate. That is the deal. If you accept it, you'll enter the Academy tomorrow. You will, however, be cuffed during your training and will not be able to leave the grounds. If you attempt to circumvent this, then the deal will be dissolved. In the event this occurs, you'll be brought straight to the council for sentencing. Do you understand?"

"Why are you doing this? You never wanted me. You never wanted a daughter. I left so we could both be free, so why the fuck can't you just let me go?"

His expression was unreadable, distant, as usual. "There is no escape from heritage, Indigo. You were born a Justice, and you will die a Justice, and it's my job as your parent to make sure your life and death honor that name."

I could call his bluff. Tell him to stick his deal and take my chances with the trial, but hell, there was no upside to that. They'd probably execute me as an example. My father had played a dangerous game to get me here, one that probably involved greasing palms and making promises, and if I went against him now, I'd be throwing myself to the mercy of the members of the council that hated him. Hated the Justices. Because despite being the crème de la crème of society, we were also the most despised.

A hollow pit yawned inside me.

After all this time.

After all the running.

He had me. He had me where he wanted me.

I exhaled heavily and met his eyes. "When do I leave?"

TWO

The human was staring at me, head tipped to the side to expose a savaged throat, mouth open and filled with blood.

"I've never been bitten before." He gurgled. "Will it hurt?"

My hands tamped down over the wound. "Sorry, so sorry. I didn't mean it. I didn't mean to hurt you. I couldn't stop. Just couldn't stop." Tears stung my eyes and kissed my cheeks. "Please, please, don't die."

"Too late, Indigo." My father's voice poured out of the human's mouth. "You did it again. You disappointed us all. You always disappoint. And you wonder why I can't love you."

Always disappoint. Never loved. Never ...

"Wake up, Indie."

A hand landed on my shoulder and had the audacity to give it a shake.

Fuck off was the desired response, but the word that came out was *harrumph*.

"Indie, come on. You promised you wouldn't miss today."

Today? Oh, yeah, the team exercise, as in *there is no I in team*, as in I didn't give a shit. But the exam was the last lesson of the evening, and my bio clock told me the sun had only just set.

Still, Minnie's shadow loomed over me, and the heat of her gorgon glare burned holes in the back of my head.

"The whole day, Indie. You promised to do a whole day," she reminded me with that stern edge to her tone, which told me that ten-inch-thick steel would break before she would.

Me and my big mouth. Maybe if I faked sickness, she'd piss off and leave me be. Going to shitty classes was the last thing I wanted to do tonight.

I coughed and made a gagging sound.

"Nah-uh," she said. "The whole frickin' day and the exam. You skip the test, and we all get a fail. And you don't want me to fail, do you?"

Urgh. Emotional blackmail, which coming from anyone else I'd be immune to. I rolled onto my back and stared at the pixie-cute woman looking down at me. Her crimson bob grazed her delicate jaw as she leaned over me, and her wide jade eyes were hard with determination.

Over the last two months, I'd learned three things

about Minnie Faraday. First, she wasn't a stuck-up arsehole like the rest of the Faraday family. Second, she had a soft spot for kittens, and anything small and furry, and third—the most important—she did not take no for an answer.

Trust me, I'd tried to keep her at a distance. I mean, sharing a room with her didn't mean we had to be friends. I didn't need or want any friends here. But Minnie had decided that's exactly what we were going to be, and she'd pursued me unrelentingly until she'd worn me down.

So, here we were. Two friends in a glare-off. One I knew I was about to lose, because yeah, I'd promised not to skip out on the simulation today. Team exercises were graded based on team performance; if one member was a no-show, the whole team suffered.

I closed my eyes and blew out a breath. "Fine. Give me five minutes, and I'll meet you in the lobby.

"Five." She narrowed her eyes. "I'll be back to get you if you don't show."

I flashed my teeth at her. "Have I ever let you down, pixie-boo?"

"Do not call me that." She crossed her arms. "You know I hate it." She sniffed.

"Riiight. So, you just wrote it in the back of your notebook and decorated it with tiny flowers for no reason then?"

She opened and closed her mouth a couple of times and then took a deep breath. "Five minutes."

She grabbed her book bag and headed out of the room.

The door didn't slam behind her.

Not too pissed off then.

Good.

I threw back the covers and swung my legs out of bed. God, I hated evenings. The moon was high and round and clearly visible through our room window. Other supernaturals struggled to adjust to the fact that we slept during the day and studied at night. But this was standard fare for a nightblood. We were nocturnal, not because the sun would fry us, but because it stripped us of our supernatural abilities, weakening us and making us easier to kill. It's where the whole kill-the-nightblood-by-day myth came from. The whole stake in the heart and all that shit. Try and stake a nightblood through the heart when the moon was up, and you'd find yourself armless. Ha. Armless. Un*armed*. Dis*armed*.

God, I needed caffeine.

But seriously, it's why we were perfect for the Nightwatch because the Watch operated mostly under cover of dark. Super cliché if you asked me.

The moonkissed adjusted easily, but the weavers and feybloods struggled. Fuck 'em, they decided they wanted to be here, so let them deal with it.

Oh, crap, I had less than two minutes to get to the lobby. Inner monologues were such a time suck. Looked like a shower would have to wait.

HAIR PULLED BACK in a messy bun, tatty sweater, jeans, and boots on—because like hell was I wearing the regulation black skirt and maroon blouse with the Academy logo—I headed out of the room and down the corridor leading to the main staircase.

The Academy was an imposing gothic building with high arches and finicky-looking fleur-de-lis slapped across every fucking surface. The dark wood and stone weren't exactly insulation friendly, and only two wings had been adapted with central heating. Because nightbloods and moonkissed didn't feel the chill like other supernaturals, we'd been shoved in the old wing where showers had to be taken in communal shower rooms. His and hers, thank God. I was no prude, but showering with male moonkissed on a full moon was asking for a hairy eyeful.

The feyblood and weavers were on the opposite side of the Academy with hot water on tap and radiators to keep them toasty warm. The final wing was reserved for shadow cadets, the prestigious males who *emerged* after drinking from the ceremonial goblet and activating their super gene. These men were marked for greatness. At least that's what the Watch told them. In truth, they were cannon fodder for the fight beyond the mist. The fight against an ancient race called fomorians who were intent on getting into our world.

The fortress, a mile away from the Academy, housed shadow knights who patrolled the tear in the fabric of our reality and ensured that didn't happen. I felt sorry for the shadow cadets. As soon as they were marked, their lives were over.

A lance of moonlight slipped through the high windows and lit up the cuffs on my wrist as I made my way down the main staircase to the huge central foyer that connected all the wings. Yeah, maybe I should focus on my own problems rather than those of a bunch of men who believed they were special.

"Nice outfit, Justice," a snide male voice called out from behind me.

Thomas Carmichael, nightblood, and stuck-up ass. I glanced over my shoulder. "Thanks, you want to borrow it?"

"Not until she fucking showers." Harmon, a moonkissed big, hairy dude, appeared behind the nightblood.

The two guys were inseparable, if you know what I mean. Although nightblood law forbade us from procreating with other species or marrying them. The rules on messing around were fuzzy, and things at the Academy were pretty relaxed.

"I can fucking smell her from here," Harmon complained, nostrils flaring as he took another long whiff.

I smirked up at him. "You're taking a nice long drag

there, Harmon. Strange for someone who finds my odor distasteful."

Heightened senses were the norm at the Academy, but the full moon meant Harmon was running on special juice tonight.

"Are my pheromones making you horny?" I fluttered my lashes at him.

Thomas bared his teeth at me, fangs on display. Everyone knew Harmon swung both ways. He wasn't subtle about it. Monogamy wasn't his strong suit, so this was Thomas staking his claim on the huge hunk of hairy meat, not that I'd ever go there.

The fact they'd spoken to me at all was kind of a shock. The cadets had steered clear of engaging with me up until now. I was, after all, there against my will —the cuffs on my wrists made that clear.

The Academy was located in a pocket of reality warded by powerful weaver magic, and there was no escape without authorized use of one of the weaver portals. But at least the other cadets knew they could get that authorization to leave, to go home to their families during the term break. But the cuffs on my wrist told them I was a prisoner. That using the portals would fry my insides. It told them that despite being a Justice—a member of one of the legacy families—I wasn't good enough.

Luckily, that was something that had been drummed into me from birth, so the scathing looks and derisive glances did shit to me.

The cuffs made me a pariah, and I was good with that.

Minnie was the exception. But then I got the impression Minnie was used to flying in the face of convention and getting what she wanted. The woman was born to be a leader, and although I'd never openly admit it, I was glad she'd decided she wanted me as a friend.

The tedium of the Academy was alleviated with her by my side.

And there she was, pointy-chinned face turned up to greet me, smile firmly in place.

"Okay, let's get this over with." I fell into step beside her as we made our way to the study wing where all the classes and labs were based.

She shot me a sly look. "You know, if you relax and allow yourself to, you might even enjoy being here."

Anger flared in my chest. "I'll go to a few classes, Min, but I'm not going to enjoy it. This wasn't the plan for my life. I do not want to be here. Remember that." There was a harsh edge to my tone, one I hadn't used with her for weeks. But she needed to understand that my feelings about my incarceration weren't about to change.

She was silent as we joined the bustle of uniformed bodies pouring into the study wing, and just when I thought she'd dropped the subject...

"What was your plan anyway? Huh?" she asked. "Pit fights and slumming it? Was that your dream?

Wouldn't it be better to accept this? Maybe they'll waive the cuffs, and you'll be able to go home to your family during the break?"

She had no idea. No idea what home had been like. What being a daughter to a man who'd wanted a son was like, or how cold the bosom of my family was.

It wasn't something I wanted to share with her, or anyone, for that matter.

I bit back my annoyance. "How about we focus on the lessons, eh, seeing as you want to ace them so bad."

I steered her toward the first class. History of Supernaturals 101. We passed a set of huge double windows open to let in the night air, and the *clank* and *chink* of metal on metal drifted up to greet us.

I couldn't help it. I had to see. There they were, shadow cadets in training armor, second years if the color of their breast plates was anything to go by. They sparred in twos, back and forth, stab, parry, thrust. Moonlight glanced off the metal surfaces of their armor and impressive weapons. No training swords there.

A huge hulking figure stood off to one side, arms crossed over his broad chest, shorn dark hair glinting silver in the moonlight, biceps bulging obscenely as if trying to escape the confines of the tight long-sleeved black top he was wearing.

Archer Hyde – the man, the legend himself. My gaze dropped to his legs, but even with my nightblood vision, it was impossible to spot which one was real and which one was mechanical from this far away. But I'd heard the stories of his battle-scarred face and formidable fighting skills. And the loss of the limb? Well, the story was that a fomorian hound had eaten his leg. He'd fought it, killed it, and carried a man back through the mist to safety. And how did the Watch repay him? By benching him and giving him a class of snotty shadow cadets to train.

One of the shadow cadets paused and glanced up at the window. He brushed his fair hair off his forehead before raising a hand in greeting.

I almost responded.

But he wasn't waving at me. He was waving at his sister. Minnie waved back, and he smiled. His gaze tracked to me, and the smile dropped, leaving only icy contempt.

Yeah. Lloyd was not happy that his little sister was besties with a Justice. I tore my gaze away and across the neatly trimmed grounds, over the tops of the gray, bushy trees to the building that rose up to touch the stars. The shadow knight fortress was an impressive structure built as a stronghold. It was also the final destination for every shadow cadet.

That would be their prison. Look at them fighting to get there.

Idiots.

"Come on," Minnie said. "We're going to be late."

I pushed away from the window ledge and joined

her in the throng of students headed to class. "You think Barnaby will notice?"

She snort-chuckled. "Probably not."

Someone bumped me and then shot me a filthy look. I bared my teeth and growled, and she hurried away.

"Seriously, Indie, do you have to be so feral?"

"Yes."

Minnie shook her head and led the way into Barnaby's class. Most tutors preferred we call them by their last names and stick Master or Madam on the front, but not Barnaby. Barnaby wanted to be hip and trendy. Problem was, he had a narcolepsy problem and spent most of the class asleep. Minnie usually took over and handed out the worksheets or handouts.

Why not report him?

What? And be given a tutor who actually stayed awake to teach? *Pffft*. With Barnaby asleep, we got to run through the sheets in fifteen and spend the rest of the hour chatting.

I guess today wasn't going to be so bad after all.

Except instead of the usual murmur of conversation, there was dead silence, and instead of Barnaby at the desk, there was a man I'd never seen before.

He looked up as we entered.

"You're late." He glanced down at the register in his hand.

In all the weeks I'd been there, I don't think Barnaby had touched that register once.

Harmon and Thomas grinned from their seats. Fuckers had beaten us there.

"Name," the man asked.

"Minnie Faraday and Indigo Justice," Minnie replied for the both of us.

The man tensed. It was a fraction of a second and then gone. He looked up, his expression smooth, and then his gaze fell on me and remained there for a little too long. He wasn't old, probably the same age as my father. But whereas my father's hair was graying at the temple, there seemed to be no gray woven into this man's thick head of golden hair. Gray eyes regarded me steadily. Okay, this was getting weird.

"Do I have something on my face?" I touched my cheek.

He blinked sharply as if snapping out of a trance. "Sit."

Wow, okay. We took our seats as he vacated his. "Master Decker is on leave for the next week, so I'll be taking this class. For those of you who don't know me, my name is Carter Payne, and I'll be your tutor for Defense Against Weaving next term." He picked up Barnaby's notebook. "Let's go over what you've been learning."

Someone snickered.

"Something funny, Samuel?" Master Payne snapped.

The feyblood in question snapped his mouth closed.

There was something imposing and commanding about this tutor. I ducked my head and focused on the grain of the wood of my desk. The sooner this class was over, the better.

"Looks like you covered history of supernatural species," he continued. "You've touched on the history of the mist. Good. So, what can you tell me?"

There was silence, and my scalp prickled in awareness and foreboding.

I raised my chin, and sure enough, his gaze was zeroed on me.

THREE

"Miss Justice. What can you tell us about the mist?" Master Payne asked.

Minnie cursed softly under her breath, probably worried I hadn't been paying attention. But me? I was like a sponge.

I sat back in my seat and straightened my legs out under my desk. "What would you like to know?"

He offered me a close-lipped smile. "How about you start from the beginning. What is the mist?"

"Um, Master Payne," Minnie interrupted. "May I?"

Carter Payne didn't even look at her. "No, you may not."

I smiled thinly before replying to his question. "The mist is a phenomenon caused by the tear in the fabric of our reality and cuts our world off from the fomorian realm. A long time ago, an ancient race called fomorians came into the human world and shacked up with supernaturals, sowing their wild oats."

Someone snickered—probably Samuel.

Master Payne glared over my head for a beat. "Please continue, Miss Justice."

I traced a pattern on my desk with an index finger. "They hoped to take over our world. To birth an army right here under our noses. But the males born with the fomorian gene decided they liked this world as it was, and when the tear appeared and the war was imminent, they turned on the fomorians and formed the order of the shadow knights. Together with the Nightwatch, they fought back the threat. We won. The fortress and Academy were built here, to train the next generation of enforcers to police the supernatural world in the mortal realm and to find the next generation of shadow knights."

When I finished speaking, the room was deathly silent. Shit. Had I gone all eloquent?

Master Payne smiled smugly, which irritated the fuck out of me. Like what the hell did he have to be smug about? I'd answered the question.

I shot Minnie a sideways glance to catch her staring at me.

"Well said, Miss Justice," Master Payne said. "Now, who can tell me about the feybloods' heritage?"

The spotlight was off me, which was what I'd wanted. So, why did I feel so annoyed?

"Well, he certainly grilled the class." Thomas shoved past us, eager to get away from the classroom.

"Watch it!" Minnie snapped.

He spun to face us and bowed. "So sorry, *ladies*. No, let me amend that, lady and tramp."

One of these days, he was going to get acquainted with my fists.

"He's not a weaver," Minnie said.

"Huh? Thomas?"

"No, Carter Payne. His powers were nullified by the shadow knight gene."

We made our way to the next class, riding the wave of students who filled the corridors with every bell. Chatter rose up around us, but it was easy to tune it out.

"That shit is true?" I shot her an incredulous look.

"Yep." Minnie shouldered her way through a knot in the crowd.

Everything was fucking legacy in our world. Legacy nightblood families and legacy weaver families. Even the moonkissed had their pack hierarchy. Payne was one of the three legacy weaver families. Nightbloods were forbidden to procreate with anyone other than nightbloods, and it was the same for weavers. The three weaver families intermarried to keep the weaver gene strong, because without weavers, magic would be lost. They were prized by the Nightwatch, and Payne had lost that power by being born with the shadow knight gene. It was rare in weaver families, and when it happened, the man was usually shunned by his peers. Marriage was out of the question.

"Why isn't he a shadow knight?"

Minnie shrugged. "I guess you'd have to ask him that. As far as I know, he's been a tutor here forever. He teaches and also runs the med bay. Not that anyone ever gets sick. I heard he uses it as a lab for his alchemy experiments."

Sounded boring. "Not interested. Let's get some food."

As we made our way toward the canteen, my mind wandered back to the system and everything that was broken. I couldn't wait to finish my sentence here and get out.

THE CANTEEN WAS the communal hub of this place, sporting a lounge area and an upper balcony heaving with books and nooks where you could curl up and read. The food was varied to accommodate the various supernatural species of cadet, and the atmosphere was thick with activity. Unlike my old nightblood school, there were no real cliques here.

The Watch had a no-tolerance policy for that kind of mentality. We were training to be Nightwatch, and that meant working together as a team whether you were nightblood, moonkissed, or feyblood. Unnatural if you ask me. Like was drawn to like, and once these cadets got out of this artificial environment, they'd go back to their prejudices. Nightbloods had a natural aversion to moonkissed and vice versa. And the feybloods that went here thought they were better than everyone else because they were descended from the shining people.

Outside, they'd be called bastardized fey. But use that term in here, and you were asking for a disciplinary.

At least the queue for food wasn't too long. My stomach rumbled as we lined up with our trays.

Minnie grabbed an apple, and I did the same even though there was no way that was hitting the spot for me today.

"You need blood," Minnie said.

We got to the moonkissed woman who was serving. She raked us over. "Type?"

"Two O neg, please," Minnie said. "Heated."

"Not for me." I held up a hand. "I'm fine."

"Are you sick?" Minnie asked. "You didn't take any blood yesterday either. You're going to get weak if you don't drink, and you need to be on the ball for the exam."

She was right, of course, but bagged blood tasted shit. "Fine." I gave the server a tight smile. "Two bags it is."

The woman ambled off to get the blood. She

returned a minute later and plonked the bags on our trays.

The smell made my stomach clench with need, but the taste would be slightly too metallic and off. Still, it was all we'd be getting here, and it was all I deserved.

We broke away from the queue and headed toward our usual table.

"Min!" A blonde, curly-haired bombshell intercepted us. "You didn't show to the pamper evening last night." She pouted. "We missed you."

Harper Bourne, feyblood legacy family, spoilt princess, and in any other environment would have been the mean girl. But in adherence to the rules of the Academy, she'd toned it down. The girls she hung with would have been called her clique, but here, they were merely her *friends*. They wore matching bubblegum lipstick and flicky eyeliner.

Fucking clones.

Made me wonder how they'd deal with the outside world when they were forced to roll around in the mud wrestling a demon dog.

Harper kept her attention on Minnie, not even bothering to acknowledge me. Nothing new there. If not for Minnie, I'd probably be invisible in this place. Trust me. I'd tried.

"We did face masks and nails." Harper wiggled her crimson-tipped fingers at Minnie. "It wasn't the same without you."

Minnie arched a brow. "Yeah, well, I decided to watch Lunar Creek with Indie instead."

The Supernatural Television Network broadcasted the show on a closed network only accessible by supernaturals, and the show was a fan favorite. Set in a coastal town with mermaids and sirens, moonkissed and nightbloods, it was a soap opera not many would miss.

"Oh, God. Klayton is sooo dreamy," one of the bubblegum posse swooned.

Harper ignored her, keeping her attention on Minnie. "Oh, you could have done that with us."

"I know." Minnie smiled stiffly. "So could Indie. If you'd bothered inviting her."

Oh, man. The urge to face-palm was almost too much.

Harper's eyes widened, and no, she still didn't look at me. "Oh, we just thought it could be us girls, you know."

"And what's Indie? Chopped liver?" Minnie shook her head. "Forget it, Harper. You haven't even said hello to her, and she's standing right here. I don't have time for bitchiness."

My friend strode off, and I made to follow.

"You're bringing her down, you know," Harper said.

It took a moment to register that she was talking to me, and another split second to register what she was implying.

I should have walked away. It would have been the

smart thing to do. But my temper overrode my common sense.

I turned slowly to face her. "You have a problem with me, then say it. Let's get it out in the open."

Her chest rose and fell, and her minions clustered around her like pink fluffy bats.

"You're a criminal," she snapped.

"So is the amount of makeup you're wearing."

She opened and closed her mouth, and then her eyes narrowed. "Problem with Minnie is her heart's too big. She's always taking in strays and nursing sick animals back to health. You're just another project to her, Justice. She doesn't realize how toxic you are. But I know about your stint in the slums, the pit fights, and the drinking."

My pulse beat faster. Did she know what my crime was? That was closed case information.

"I'll find out what you did, and once I do—"

"You'll what?" Minnie reappeared sans tray. "I don't care about the past. I care about the here and now. Everyone has a right to a second chance."

My chest tightened with dread. If she knew the truth ...

"Come on, Indie, blood's getting cold."

She wove her arm through mine and tugged me away from Harper and her posse.

We took our seats at our regular corner table, and I pushed away the feeling of dread.

"I'm way too old for this shit, you know." I picked

up my blood bag. "You'd think at our age, we'd be past all this petty crap."

"Eighteen is hardly old in nightblood years," Minnie said.

"Nineteen. I'll be nineteen next month."

She licked her lips and leaned in. "Want to know a secret?"

"Like I'm going to say no to that."

Her eyes twinkled. "Harper is twenty-five. She went through a rebel phase when she was younger, and then her parents grounded her for a year before pulling strings to get her in last year. They've threatened to cut her off if she doesn't shape up."

"And hanging out with a Faraday helps."

She shrugged and winked. "Eat up, we have an exam to ace."

THE NEXT CLASS was on the upper floor situated next to a room that hummed with the whirr of machinery and blinking lights. The tiny room powered the Sim lab where pods were grouped into scrums of six. Most of the cadets hovered by the windows on the far end of the room, looking nervous.

Not surprising. The pods took some getting used to. My first time had resulted in ten minutes of vomiting. But after several trials over the past eight weeks, because like hell did anyone get to lie low in this class, my brain had acclimatized to being hooked up to a machine so my consciousness could be beamed to a simulated location. Even so, my stomach did a little flip of nerves.

"Why can't we just do the test in the real world?" a young feyblood male asked.

Pale, tall, broad-shouldered, and typically beautiful – which meant he was a Tuatha mixed with some other supernatural breed—the guy drew every eye with his question.

The Tuatha were always too good-looking to be real. This one was twirling a strand of his gleaming shoulder-length, silver-blond hair around his finger while fluttering his impossibly long eyelashes at Madam Garnet, the sim tutor.

Out in the real world, maybe Garnet and I would have been friends. Short and stocky, she had the don't-mess-with-me attitude I admired and was my favorite tutor here – if I gave a shit about favorites.

"Why can't we do this outside?" She glared at him. "Do we have fomorian hounds and rogue fey running around the bloody academy that I don't bloody know about?"

He opened his mouth to reply, but she cut him off. "No. No, we do not, and you know why? Because this is a bloody secure location." She crossed her arms. "These pods are as close as you get to a supernatural threat until your third term, and let's hope by that time you're ready to face the challenge." She tapped the holotab in her hand. "The pods, for those of you that need a reminder, are Feytech, which means they are infallible, unbreakable, and un ... damn, I can't think of another word."

"Perfect?" Harmon offered, his attention on a curvy female moonkissed.

Thomas's face pinched.

"No, Harmon," Madam Garnet said. "That wasn't the word I was looking for. How about you bloody stick to finishing Carmichael's sentences."

A low chuckle rippled across the class.

Garnet ignored them. "The pods will keep you safe while you're linked to the sim arena. Like anything that comes from Winterlock Tech, these pods have been tested and retested. Only the best for our cadets." She tapped several buttons. "Teams are ..."

She began to rattle off names, reiterating what we already knew.

"Minnie Faraday, Harmon Black, Thomas Carmichael, Indigo Justice, and Oberon Hyde."

My pulse skipped. Hyde? Like Archer Hyde. They were spawned directly from Orion Winterlock's bloodline – the only pure-blood fey on the mortal realm, council member, and owner of Winterlock Tech. Orion had certainly sown his oats, but the Hydes were the only feyblood line that were both descended from Orion and made up of a mix of human and fey genes. It made them more fey than any other feybloods because human genes were recessive to fey genes.

The golden-haired feyblood inclined his head, his gaze sliding our way. Whereas a moment ago, his expression had been airhead, now it was sly and cunning. What the actual fuck?

"Shit," Minnie said. "Oberon sucks and not in a nice way."

Thomas groaned as if he was hearing the news about our team-up for the first time, but I was pretty sure his objection wasn't to Oberon. His next words confirmed it.

"Come on, Madam. Why do we have to be stuck with the criminal?"

My neck heated, but I kept a straight face and my eyes on the whiteboard behind Garnet.

Garnet lowered her holotab and fixed her eyes on Thomas. "Are you questioning my judgment?" Her tone was a knife's edge.

Thomas pressed his lips together. "Of course not."

Her smile was brittle as she turned her attention to me. "I'm sure Miss Justice knows better than to let the team down."

I didn't bother gracing her with a response, verbal or otherwise, and after a long, uncomfortable stare-off, she returned her attention back to the class.

"The past eight weeks, you've been learning about the kind of threats you'll be facing back in the human world. Threats from your own kind, from rogue nightbloods and moonkissed, from feybloods and creatures that enter our world via thinnings in our reality. The fomorians aren't the only threat to our world, and although some of you will find yourselves chosen to fight the bigger threat, the rest of you will be rooted in the mortal world, fighting every day to keep the universal glamour from failing by making sure our existence remains secret. To do that, you'll need to bring down the trouble-makers, the rogues, and the factions that care little for the balance of things. You'll need to police demons that enter our world in an unauthorized fashion. You are the only line of defense beyond these wards." She took a deep breath. "So, show me what you've learned. Work together in your teams to survive. Use the tools in your pack to get from point A to B, and remember, you need to cross that finish line together. If you lose a member or leave one behind, you all fail."

Shit, this was not going to be fun.

"Well, what are you waiting for? Fire up, and let's get this exam underway."

Harmon and Thomas ambled over to us. As a team, we needed to be in connected pods. There were five of us, so one pod would be vacant. Oberon appeared at my side.

"Mind if I take the spot next to you?"

It was the first time he'd spoken to me, and his voice was like honey. I hated honey.

"Do what you want." I climbed into my pod and hit the calibration controls.

The material of the seat was soft and alive as it

molded to my body. Around me, the others hurried to get settled. I pressed my head back against the rest and closed my eyes. Don't hold your breath. Don't ...

Shit, the material whooshed over my head, covering it entirely in a semi-permeable material that I didn't know the name of. The first time this had happened, I'd almost passed out from hyperventilating, and then there'd been the puke. Yeah, all over my face.

I'd have been mortified if I'd been the only one chucking up my guts. Pod riding took time to adjust to.

Shit, hurry up already.

My head felt light, and then the world was whooshing away.

FOUR

I opened my eyes in a leafy clearing at night. The air smelled crisp and clean, like just after a heavy rainfall, except the ground was bone dry.

Little incongruences like this ruined the authenticity of the simulation.

I looked up at the night sky and studied the map of stars—one map I could always navigate by—except it was all off. Urgh. Could they not get anything right? It shouldn't bother me, but it did. Maybe I should say something; surely these tests should be more realistic with a little more attention to detail?

Why did I even care?

"Hey?" Minnie appeared beside me, a huge grin on her pixie face. "I have a good feeling about this test."

I couldn't help but smile back. It felt strange on my face. Smiling. "Are you sure you're a Faraday?"

She snorted. "Not all Faradays are sticks-in-the-butt."

"Except your uncle and your brother."

She winced. "Lloyd has his moments. He's under a lot of pressure to be ... perfect."

Yeah, if anyone understood pressure, it was me. I'd grown up under the pressure of being the wrong sex.

I took in Minnie's outfit: combat trousers with a dagger strapped to the thigh, long-sleeved, dark-green top, and heavy-duty boots. Mine was the same. Clothes designed to blend in, and shoes made to carry us over difficult terrain. One thing she had that I didn't was a backpack. It sat snug against her back and bulged with items.

I guess Minnie was the resource manager then.

Harmon and Thomas strode toward us from the tree line. They were dressed the same as us. Thomas wore the outfit easily, his slender form looking comfortable in the getup, but Harmon? Not so much. The pants looked too tight, and his polo top stretched, ready to burst at the seams.

He tugged at the collar. "It's a simulation, you'd think they'd get the proportions right."

I rolled my eyes. "We're in a simulation, so you're not actually wearing the clothes. There's no reason for them to get it right."

Something made an eerie chirping sound.

"You think they'd be a little more original when it comes to location," Thomas said drolly.

"Would you rather we were in a desert?" Minnie asked.

"At least then we'd see any danger coming," Thomas replied.

"We'd probably die of thirst and exposure first," Harmon said. "Come on, Tom, think." His tone was good-natured, but there was no mistaking the glint of annoyance in Thomas's eyes.

It looked like there was trouble in paradise.

"Where's golden boy?" I glanced about, searching for Oberon.

The clearing was obviously the rendezvous spot, so he should have been dropped close by.

"Fuck him," Harmon said.

"I bet you would," Thomas muttered under his breath.

But he might as well have shouted it—we all had super hearing, after all.

Harmon's chest rumbled. "What the fuck is that supposed to mean?"

Thomas exhaled through his nose and closed his eyes. "Nothing. It means nothing. We should get moving."

Honestly, these guys. "You want to fail? I mean not that I give a shit, but I assume you guys do."

They looked at me with matching frowns.

"We have to wait for him," Minnie said. "Teamwork, remember? If we leave anyone behind, we lose."

"Fuck." Harmon rubbed the back of his neck. "Fine, let's go find him. Maybe this is part of the test. Maybe he's in trouble?"

It was a possibility.

Just then Oberon strolled into the clearing, cargo pants hugging his slender hips, hair pulled back off his chiseled face in a half pony, sapphire eyes cool as they took us in.

"So, are we going to go somewhere?" He shrugged. "Or do you plan on hanging out in the clearing until they drag us out of the sim?"

Irritation flared in my chest. "What took you so long, Goldie? Did you stop for some porridge?"

He pouted at me and I gave him the finger.

"We have to get to this spot." Minnie waved a map around. "Look."

Animosity aside, we gathered around to stare at the map.

Map reading wasn't my forte. Everything looked the same to me, and the Geographical History of Supernaturals on Human Realms class was my go-to place for a nap. The tutor, Master Braun, had a voice that could tame the wildest hellhound and put it into a coma. He also happened to have a face like a hellhound, but that was beside the point.

Yeah, so maps were not my strong suit.

Minnie, however, was in her element.

She tucked her hair behind her ears, which, with her pixie features, should have been pointed. But nightbloods didn't have pointy ears. Wait, what did she just say?

"It looks like a twenty-mile hike," Thomas said.

"Yes," Minnie agreed. "The forest stretches for ten miles, and then we have flatlands that bleed to mountainous terrain, and finally, the body of water we're headed toward." She tapped a red X marked on the map. "Here. We have to get here."

"In the middle of the water?" Oberon said, brow crinkled.

I sighed. "It's probably a small island. There'll be a boat."

"Unless they expect us to swim," Thomas added.

Minnie opened the pack so we could examine the items. "Water purification tablets, energy bars, a tarp, an empty flask – looks like we have to get our own water – oh, and a pouch filled with green goop."

"Healing everness. Nice," Harmon said. "Should knit wounds if we get hurt. Which I do not plan to do."

"Okay, so we have basic shit," Thomas said. "I'll carry it."

Minnie finished putting everything back into the bag and then hauled it onto her shoulders. "I've got it," she said tersely.

God, we were a fucked-up bunch.

I broke away from the group. Now that Minnie had read the map and pointed out the path, it was burned in my mind.

"Let's get this over with." I set off. "I'm already bored."

Minnie jogged to catch up to me as I crossed the clearing and dove into the gloom of the forest proper. Sounds erupted around me—chirps and shuffles and the smell of life. Okay, this was good stuff. I almost believed this was real.

"We'll need to make camp before the sun comes up," Minnie said.

"Why?"

"Because ... Because we'll be vulnerable."

"And you think sleeping during the daytime, out in the open, is safe?" I gave her a flat look.

"Hate to say it," Harmon said gruffly. "But killer here is right."

Killer? My chest tightened, and my skin prickled. I could imagine the blood draining from my face. How could he know? The council had promised to keep the reason for my sentence a secret.

Maybe it was just a figure of speech? But still ... "Don't fucking call me that." My voice cracked.

"Why not?" Thomas said. "It's true, isn't it?"

Okay, not a figure of speech. "You don't have a fucking clue."

"Then fill us in," Thomas pushed.

Nothing was sacred. Nothing off the table. He was a Carmichael. Nephew to council member Carmichael, and nightbloods loved to gossip.

He knew.

He knew the truth, and he'd told his hairy boyfriend.

Heat flooded my limbs, and my hands curled into fists. "I'll fill your face with my fist if you don't shut the hell up."

Beside me, Minnie had gone silent. My pulse spiked. Had she known? No, she hadn't. What if she didn't want to be friends now?

A vise squeezed my lungs. No problem. She was a pain anyway. I'd never wanted to be friends.

Her hand nudged my arm, and then her fingers wrapped around mine and squeezed.

The vise relaxed.

"Shit happens," Minnie said softly. "Like I said, everyone deserves a second chance." She smiled up at me, then glared at Thomas. "Drop it."

Thomas blew out an exasperated breath. "Fine. But I think we have a right to know if she's about to go bloodlust on us."

"Why? You think she'll be gunning for your throat?" Minnie drawled.

Blood was blood when under the influence of bloodlust. But the episode that had resulted in my killing a human had been engineered, not that I could prove it.

My tone was clipped. "I wouldn't touch you with a ten-foot pole, Carmichael."

"What about me?" Oberon said from beside me. His arm brushed mine. He was a head taller than me and smelled of flowers. "I hear feyblood blood is intoxicating to nightbloods."

I needed him to back off. His scent was messing with my head. "I wouldn't know."

He leaned in. "You want to find out?"

I glared up at him. "Do not flirt with me, flower boy. I will hurt you."

"Yeah, I heard you had a temper," Thomas said.

I exhaled to release the rising anger.

We climbed over a fallen log, boots crunching on dry bracken.

He chuckled. "The black sheep of the Jus—"

My fist met his jaw. He staggered back clutching his face, eyes blazing.

"What the fuck?" Harmon charged me, and I dropped into a defensive crouch, ready to rumble, blood bubbling with the need to let off steam and shut down the voices in my head that screamed *murderer*. Physical pain worked well to mask the guilt, to assuage it a little.

"Enough!" Minnie stepped between us and slammed her hands into Harmon's chest. "Touch her, and you'll be answering to me."

Harmon's chest heaved as he looked down on Minnie.

She was small, she was cute, and she wouldn't need to get her hands dirty. The Faradays were connected, and her brother was a shadow cadet.

Harmon backed off. "Keep a leash on your crazy friend, Faraday."

I stepped around Minnie. "And you keep a leash on your lover's tongue."

Thomas had recovered. Not even any bruising. Shame. But we nightbloods healed quick.

Oberon clapped his hands together. "As fun as getting to know you all is, I'd rather get this exercise over with. There's a party in the real world tonight, one I don't intend to miss."

"Shit," Harmon said. "I promised to run with the guys. Full moon and all that." He scratched his stubbled face. "I say we call a truce. No baiting." He looked at Thomas, who glared back at him with dark, angry eyes. "Let's focus on the task, eh?"

Who knew the big lug could be the voice of reason when he wasn't busy sticking his cock into the next available hole?

We turned back to the trail we'd stumbled on and had barely gone five meters when the smell of copper hit my nostrils.

Animal blood.

"Whoa, that's strong," Thomas said, bringing a hand up to cover his nose.

Yeah, he'd probably never fed off anything but human blood, never had to scavenge to survive. I wondered how he'd take to rat blood. Bile climbed up my throat. Never again.

Howls filled the air.

Harmon growled low before falling into a crouch, knuckles grazing the ground.

Oberon cursed softly under his breath.

Animal blood meant there was a predator about.

Looked like we were about to face our first challenge.

FIVE

"Those are moonkissed howls," Harmon said. "I can smell them, but they smell ... off."

"Of course they do," Thomas said. "This is a test, so they're probably rogue. Shit, they've probably been feeding off humans." His eyes widened in horror.

"Delirium pack?" Minnie said, mouth set in a grim line. "We need to get out of here. We can skirt around them, and—

"Help! Please, help!"

The new scent hit me, and my mouth filled with saliva. "Human. Male. He's hurt ... bleeding."

"Definitely delirium," Harmon said, his expression somber.

I took several steps in the direction of the cry for help before pulling up short. What was I doing? This wasn't real.

"The task was to get from A to B," Harmon said. "We need to stick to the task."

"A to B," Thomas agreed. "This is a distraction we don't need."

"You really think that's all there is to it?" Oberon said. "We're training for the Watch here. And there's a *human* in distress."

I folded my arms under my breasts. "He's probably dead now that you guys spent so long discussing what to do."

"I say we help him," Minnie said. "It's what we're meant to do. It's what Nightwatch is all about."

No, Nightwatch was about saving our own asses. Saving humans simply contributed to this goal by maintaining the universal glamour that prevented them from seeing our true natures intact and keeping our existence a secret. But heck, what was the point in arguing.

"Indie? You with me?" Minnie asked.

Always. "Whatever. Let's stop gabbing and do something."

"Please! Help!"

I turned and headed toward the sound, and Minnie followed. The others would just have to catch up.

Branches lashed at my face, and leaves kissed my cheeks as adrenaline coursed through my limbs. We dove deeper into the forest, the smell of earth and blood mingling to make a heady concoction.

A bloodcurdling scream tore the night, and I broke into a run.

"Wait!" Thomas called from behind us. "We need to talk about this. What do we know about delirium? How do we subdue these moonkissed?"

All the fucking lessons that I'd allowed to wash over me. All the information that I'd been determined to ignore, and the answer bloomed in my mind like a slap to my will.

"We don't."

Harmon huffed as he came up beside me. "She's right, you can't subdue a delirium."

No, there was only one course of action. "We have to kill them."

SIX

Every supernatural knew what a delirium was. It was the moonkissed equivalent of bloodlust, except there was no coming out of it. Once a wolf went into delirium, it stayed there. It killed and killed again. And that was where the Nightwatch came in.

They took them down.

Despite my determination not to pay attention, that lesson had stuck. There was no imprisoning a delirium, no subduing. The Watch opted for on-the-spot execution. It was a mercy for the moonkissed.

The worst thing was a moonkissed didn't have to willingly eat human flesh to become a delirium. If a moonkissed was fed the meat unknowingly, it would still trigger the change in them, turning them into a monster trapped between human and wolf form forever.

And hungry. Always hungry.

"What's the plan?" Minnie asked no one and everyone.

There was only one way to bring them down fast. "Go for the main arteries. They're hyped up on adrenaline, heart's pumping fast. They'll bleed out quick."

"Yeah, but that means getting close." Thomas's tone was tight.

"If you're worried you can't hack it, then hang back," Oberon sneered. "We don't want to lose this test because you freak out and get your throat ripped open."

There was no time to dwell on strategy because we were barreling into a clearing to find a pack of wolves in half shift. Two of them stood under a tree to our far left, and three were hunkered down shoveling a red, gory mass into their snouted faces.

It wasn't real, and yet my body reacted by going into high alert. My brain registered the scenario and immediately switched to fight mode.

"There, up the tree." Minnie pointed at the same moment as all the delirium wolves swiveled their heads to look our way.

Shit.

A man was practically obscured by the foliage. The screamer no doubt. But we were now the new prey. Drool dripped from hairy jaws, and all-too-human eyes glared at us, rimmed red by the insanity that gripped their minds. Growls shook the clearing and fear bloomed in the back of my mind, not caring that this was part of a simulation or that these insane moonkissed couldn't physically hurt me.

The wolfmen advanced.

The daggers strapped to our thighs now made sense.

It was time to get stabby.

Fighting came naturally to me. The moves, the evasion, and the attack. My body was in vigilant mode. One eye on Minnie to make sure she was okay, the other on my opponent, who slashed with his claws and snapped with his serrated maw. Shit, did he just spatter me with saliva? Yuck. I spun-kicked him, knocking him into a tree, and followed up with a sharp jab to his jugular before he could recover.

He grabbed the wound, gurgling indignantly. But instead of hitting dirt, he lunged at me. The tips of his talons grazed my shirt, and pain lanced across my skin.

What the fuck? Pain? For real?

Shit.

I dropped and punctured his femoral artery with the dagger before rolling out of his reach.

"Indie!"

Minnie?

There she was—pinned to the ground. Beast on top of her. I was already in motion, world rushing by as I hit the wolfman from the side, knocking him off and going with him. My dagger sank between his ribs, then into his neck, once, twice. I kicked out and leapt off him.

"Indie, shit. Indie." Minnie sat up, clutching her abdomen. Her shirt was torn, and her hands were bloody. "Oh, fuck it *hurts*."

Nightbloods healed fast, but this wound was deep, and she'd bleed out before she had time to heal. The herb pouch! I needed to use the herb pouch, but the damn backpack wasn't on her back anymore.

Ignoring the ruckus, ignoring the growls and yelps, I scanned the clearing to find the pack lying by the tree line beyond the fight that was still raging.

Minnie moaned. "Why do they have to make it hurt?"

Her face was pale and beaded with sweat. They were giving her pain. I had to stop it.

She gripped my arm. "Don't you dare let me die. I cannot fail this, Indie. You know I can't."

Fucking Faraday pressure. "I won't."

Three wolfmen were down, and only two remained. Thomas and Harmon were tag-teaming one, while Oberon fought the other. Moving Minnie wasn't an option, and if one of the wolves broke free from the guys and headed her way, she was fucked. But if I didn't act, she was still fucked.

Game over.

I took in the fight, tracking the moves the guys and the wolves were making. I measured the distance between me and the backpack, using the guys as obstacles in my mind. There it was—the perfect route.

"I'll be right back, Min."

I rose, allowed my thighs to bunch, and then sprang off into the fray in super-fast nightblood mode. The world blurred as I wove through the bodies and skidded to a halt at the pack. One strap was sliced and frayed. I scooped it up by the strap that was intact and then dove back into the fray. Shoulder almost grazing Oberon's back, head ducking in time to avoid Harmon's power swing at the wolfman, I made it through the fight and skidded to my knees by Minnie.

She was breathing shallow. Her lips bloodless.

I tore the pack open, ripped the herb pouch in two, and slapped the contents all over her abdomen.

"Hey, what the fuck?" Thomas's voice cut across the suddenly silent clearing.

I guess the fight was over. I glanced over my shoulder to see Thomas approaching. He had the human by the nape and was steering him toward me.

Minnie shuddered. "I think it's working."

"*This* would have worked better." Thomas shoved the human to his knees beside us. "A few sips and she'd have healed fine. Now you've wasted the bloody herb pouch."

Realization dawned. The human was there to heal the nightbloods. Of course. An instant healing potion, which meant the herbs must have been a lifeline for Oberon and Harmon.

"Fuck."

Oberon tucked his hands into his pocket. "It's done now. No point stressing about it." His shirt was ripped in several places, showcasing toned marble abs, but his skin was unmarred—not even a scratch. He caught me looking, and his perfect lips curved in a lopsided smile. "You're not the only one with moves."

"I thought the only moves you had were the ones you made on the female population of the Academy," Thomas said snidely.

It was true. Oberon got around.

"How are you feeling?" Oberon asked, his intense gaze fixed on Minnie. "You think you can travel?"

Minnie tried to stand and then sat back down with a sharp yelp.

"We'll need to make camp," Harmon said. "Minnie needs time to heal. The herbs will take some time to work on a nightblood. They're not designed for your kind." His lip curled. "If you'd bothered to attend any of the herbology classes, you'd know this."

"So, give her the human." I jerked my thumb at the guy.

The human let out an indignant yelp.

"You would say that," Thomas said. "No qualms."

Thank God he couldn't feel how sweaty my palms were at being this close to a human. Thank goodness he didn't know that the very thought of drinking from the vein sent me into a panic.

"It's too late to offer Minnie the human," Harmon

said. "The herb will block the effects of any blood she consumes."

So, I'd fucked up. Big deal. It was just a game. Still, my cheeks warmed. "I'll gather some wood."

"Least you can do," Thomas called after me.

I flipped him the bird, but my insides were quivering. I may just have cost us the exercise. May have cost Minnie the grade she needed.

My success didn't matter, but hers did.

This time, there was no pretending I didn't care.

SEVEN

The bodies of the delirium were piled in a corner, still dead, still here in the sim. At least they hadn't disappeared and ruined the realism of the situation.

Maybe this was more authentic than I'd thought.

Minnie's pain certainly was. We'd put the tarp down for her to lie on at a safe distance from the fire Harmon had built. The hairy dude crouched by the flames, poking them with a stick every now and then. Thomas watched him, using the side-eye, and Oberon ... well, Oberon was staring at me.

I glared back at him, not bothering to hide my irritation. "What? Spit it out."

He canted his head. "Well, if you insist. I was wondering how you could possibly be related to Kat Justice."

Yeah, this was bound to come up at some point. My

older cousin was a legend in the Nightwatch. A prodigy who'd aced every exam and test and graduated with fucking wings.

I gave him a close-lipped smile. "Did you not pay attention in genetics class in lower school? Or do the feybloods not learn about that shit?"

He gave me a half smile, unfazed by my irritation. "You got the moves. You'd make a solid officer for the Watch."

"Right. Uh-huh, except I don't want to be in the Watch." I enunciated each word. "I'm here because I have to be, and I'm *here* for her." I jerked my thumb in Minnie's direction.

"You act all tough like you don't give a shit but you do. You care about Minnie," Oberon said. "I see through your façade."

What the fuck? "There is no façade. I was perfectly happy in my life before ..." I ducked my head.

"Before you killed someone?" Oberon said softly. "You didn't mean to do it, did you?" He leaned forward. "Tell us what happened."

The memory of that night, of the blood in my mouth, of the sweet taste, and then the hunger, sudden and overwhelming, and then nothing. Nothing. I fucking didn't remember anything.

"Indie?"

My head snapped up. "Don't call me that. You don't get to call me that."

He held up his hands. "I'm sorry. I just. I think if

you allow yourself to open up, you might find this is exactly where you need to be."

"Oh, my God," Thomas drawled, shooting Oberon a disgusted look. "The shit you'll say to get laid."

Was that what he was doing? Softening me up. I locked gazes with him to find him watching me with an intense expression, and then his face broke into a grin, and he shook his head.

"Hey, got to pass the time somehow."

Wanker.

The human made a choking sound. He'd been sitting quietly up until now, and I'd succeeded in ignoring his presence, but that was impossible to do if he made noise.

"You okay?" Harmon asked gruffly.

The man nodded. "Yeah, just. This is the weirdest dream I've ever had. I mean … I keep thinking I should wake up now, but I can't." He poked Thomas's arm. "So real."

Ice did a slow trickle through my veins. "You think you're dreaming?"

He blinked at me and pushed his spectacles up his nose. "Oh, yes. I went to bed, and then I was here, so it's a dream. I have vivid dreams all the time, but this one is the best so far. Although those monsters were more of a nightmare, but I was like, I need to get help, and there you were." He grinned and nodded. "Lucid dreaming. I made you guys appear, I guess. But I can't

... I can't seem to wake up." He gave an awkward little laugh.

"Fucking hell," Harmon said.

"They wouldn't." Thomas sounded unsure.

Oberon let out a wry bark of laughter. "Yeah, well, looks like they did."

The human was real. He was real, and he was in the sim.

"WHAT THE FUCK?" Thomas whispered.

We huddled a little way from the fire, one eye on the human and a sleeping Minnie.

"They took a human and stuck him in a pod." Harmon scratched his stubbled chin. "How many more?"

"One for each team, probably," Oberon said.

So, we'd established the human was not a computer-generated character, unless ... "That could just be his script."

"What?" Thomas made a face. "You mean they created him to say that?"

Oberon stood, tongue in cheek, and nodded. "It could be."

I sighed. "It doesn't matter. We're stuck with him for now. We can't leave him out here alone. It's probably part of the test, the whole *save the human* thing."

Minnie moaned and rolled onto her side. "Indie?"

I left the guys and rushed over to her. "You okay? You in pain?"

She smiled up at me. "Nah, it's gone." She ran a hand over her abdomen. "All healed."

I held my hand out to her. "In that case, let's get a move on." I hauled her up and looked up at the rapidly pinkening sky. "Looks like we'll be hiking during the day." I couldn't help but smile. "Been a long time since I saw the sun, even if it is a fake one."

Harmon kicked earth over the fire, and we were off.

IT WAS strange feeling the kiss of the sun on my skin, feeling my lungs work with exertion, and feeling my limbs tire. Harmon and Oberon were unaffected by the sun, but Thomas, Minnie, and I lagged a few meters behind the two guys.

Oberon said something, and Harmon threw back his head and laughed.

Thomas snorted derisively.

"Oh, for goodness' sake," Minnie snapped. "If it bothers you so much why continue to date him?"

Thomas's jaw clenched. "None of your business."

"It's not like you hide your feelings on Harmon's wandering eye."

It was obvious. "He's in love with him. He thinks

he'll change." It was my turn to snort. "People don't change."

"Fuck you, Justice."

"Ain't gonna happen."

"Looks like we're out of the woods," Minnie said. "Literally."

The forest opened onto flatlands, green fields, and the odd shrub or bush. Green, bright green. Colors so vivid in the warm buttery rays of the sun.

"Back home, I sometimes wake early to watch the sunset," Minnie said.

"Me too," Thomas replied with a sigh. "I went out during the day once, and my parents went insane. I got grounded for a month."

"How old were you?" Minnie asked.

He ducked his head. "Fifteen."

The Academy took cadets aged from seventeen to twenty-one and some even older if the Watch felt they'd be valuable assets or if their families happened to be legacy. But everyone did three years at the Academy unless you were a prodigy like my cousin, Kat, who'd completed all the requisite programs and exams in a year and a half.

"So, when do you think they'll throw another curveball at us?" Thomas asked.

The vista was too serene, and his words put me on edge. "Let's hope whatever it is, it's not till tonight. We'll be three men down if we get attacked again during the day."

"Look!" Harmon picked up the pace. "Fruit."

Bushes laden with colorful fruit dotted the ground ahead.

"Ah, the opportunity to gather supplies," Oberon drawled.

Thomas let out a whoop and rushed ahead.

"Not sure why he's getting so excited. It's not blood," Oberon said.

"Nightbloods eat food," Minnie said.

"But only for show," Oberon countered.

"Some of us do enjoy the taste," Minnie countered.

She was right, but our bodies weren't designed to digest it. Eating regular foods too often made us sick.

We joined the others in the grove of fruit. Oval-shaped pink fruit, and what looked like oranges but much smaller.

"I recognize these," Oberon said. "We have them at home. Mother grows them in the hothouse. Seeds from Faerie that have been cultivated over generations. This fruit is rare."

I picked one and turned it over in my hands. It had velvety skin like a peach and felt warm from the sun. Nice touch. "Are they safe to eat?"

"We have them on special occasions." Oberon shrugged.

"That doesn't mean they're safe for us." Harmon leaned in to sniff one.

Thomas was reaching for a peachy fruit but dropped his hand. "Good point."

"Come on." Harmon set off again. "We've made good time. Let's keep up the pace, and we can be at the water body by nightfall."

If I hadn't fucked up and used the herbs on Minnie instead of sticking the human under her nose, then we would already be strolling up to our mark by now. Instead, we had several more hours of walking left.

An hour later, and the human was flagging.

"We'll have to stop," Minnie said. "The human needs to rest."

"Henry, my name is Henry."

My stomach twisted in guilt. We'd pretty much ignored him, and no one had bothered to ask him his name. The whole is he real or is he a computer-generated construct was messing with all our heads.

"I need to sit," he said. And then he just dropped where he was. "Maybe if I go to sleep here, I'll wake up in my bed."

The ground had become uneven and rocky, and there was a definite incline to the terrain. We couldn't be more than an hour or so from our destination. If we kept going ...

The human groaned. "My feet ache."

"I could do with a rest," Minnie said. "This day walking is kinda tiring."

"Yeah, now I understand why we use golems to do our day bidding," Thomas said. "I can't wait to get mine once I graduate."

Golems were a luxury the legacy families got to

enjoy. Woven into existence by the head weaver and his team at Nightwatch headquarters, they were custom designed to suit their masters.

I found a flat-looking rock and parked my butt. "Fine, we take a break."

Harmon and Oberon exchanged glances and then shrugged and joined us.

"Minnie, how about one of those energy bars?" Harmon asked.

Minnie passed the energy bars to Harmon and Oberon, then retrieved the blood bags for us.

I shook my head when she offered me one. "No, thanks. I'm good."

Thomas accepted his.

"Funny?" Oberon said, eyes on the sky. "Sun's setting. Early."

"I guess someone on the outside wants to hurry us along." Thomas sucked on his blood bag. "Not bad for a simulation drink."

"How long do you think we've been under in reality?" Minnie asked.

"Couldn't be that long." I shrugged. "It's a double period, so they probably want us done in two hours."

"Hence the fast sunset." Oberon nodded. "Makes sense."

The sky pinkened and then darkened. A tingle ran over my skin as my nightblood powers surged back to the surface with the waking of the moon, but then my fingers and palm flared with prickling pain that quickly turned into a burn.

"Shit!" I shook my hand.

"You okay?" Minnie reached out to take my wrist and studied my palm. "Shit, what is that?"

Even with the rapidly setting gloom, the red smudges on my fingertips and palm were clearly visible.

"Fuck, it burns." I pulled away from her as the burn sank into my skin and was gone. "Okay, that was weird." I wiggled my fingers. "It's gone."

"What happened?" Henry asked.

I glanced over at him, suddenly hyperaware of his presence—the smell of him, the sound of his blood whooshing through his veins. My gums throbbed, and hunger squeezed my stomach.

Oh, God.

I stood and backed away.

"Indie, what is it?" Minnie reached for me, but I jerked away.

This couldn't be happening. Not now. Not again. I couldn't go through this again. But there was nothing but the thud of Henry's pulse and the gallop of my heart, nothing but the hunger. It rose up like a blanket to cloak my consciousness—a crimson tide of ravenous intent. I had to fight it. I needed to get away before it took over, before the bloodlust claimed me and I killed the human.

But there was no getting away.

We were stuck in a simulation until we passed the finish line or until we died.

Died.

My fangs elongated. The hunger was about to take over. There was only one thing to do.

I yanked the dagger from my leg holster.

"Indie? What the fuck?" Minnie said, wide-eyed.

But my vision was darkening, senses zeroed in on my prey. "I'm sorry. I just. I can't let this happen ..."

I plunged the knife into my chest.

EIGHT

Principal Brunner tapped her desk and studied me from behind her neat round spectacles. She was a minute woman with sharp, inquisitive features and pale blue eyes that seemed to peer into your soul. She was dressed in her signature long-sleeved, high-necked navy-blue shirt, hair up in a chignon and face free of any makeup. Not that she needed it. She had the clear, glowing skin that was common among the feybloods and a sweet honeysuckle scent which was probably her natural body odor.

Her office was small, sparse, and neat, just like the woman herself. Dark wood paneling was interrupted by a wall-to-wall bookcase lined with impressive-looking tomes. Two freestanding lamps parked on either side of the room lit it up in warm light. There was an old-fashioned coat rack with an umbrella stand attached, and the desk was one of those antique things, polished to such a shine that it made you afraid you might scratch it.

It was a pleasant, soothing space, and despite the knot in my stomach, I found myself relaxing. I was no stranger to being reprimanded. All that mattered was the sim was over. No more murder. I'd stopped it from happening again. No need to dwell, just shove it in a box and move on.

"Madam Garnet explained what happened in the sim," Brunner said. "The fruit you came across was another test. Only feybloods can consume it. It has strange effects on other supernaturals, bringing their worst fears to the surface."

In my case, my fear of draining a human. I took a measured breath. It was over.

She frowned. "You're afraid to hurt a human. Not the modus operandi of a killer."

"But I am a killer. I killed a human." My voice was bitter.

"On purpose?" She canted her head.

I looked away. "Intent doesn't matter. Only the outcome."

"Hmmm. Yes, I guess to the council ..." She pursed her lips. "I understand why you chose to exit. But in doing so, you've caused your teammates to fail the exam, and you've failed the class."

I stared at a point behind her, a fraying edge of the heavy cream drapes that hung at the tall window. "I'm not here to pass classes."

She frowned and sat forward. "I'm not sure I understand what you mean? You accepted the deal to come here, did you not?"

"Yeah, and I'm here. Doesn't mean I have to participate."

She made an 'o' with her mouth. "Miss Justice, I believe there's been a huge misunderstanding. As far as I was informed, your grade must remain above a C average for you to remain here. If it drops below that, then the deal your father struck with the council will be void, and you'll be handed over to the council for sentencing."

The words coming out of her mouth took a moment to register, and then panic gripped me. They hadn't said anything about grades or passing. That hadn't been the deal.

"Indigo." Brunner sat forward, her hands clasped in front of her. "At the risk of sounding cliché, you have much potential, and the only person holding you back is you. I don't want to have to hand you over to the council, but I'll have no choice if you can't keep your grades up. There are four weeks until the end-of-term exams. Your test and coursework grades are low to non-existent. If you're going to pass, then everything will ride on those end-of-term papers." She sighed and sat back. "It's up to you." She looked to the door. "You may go. I believe Miss Faraday is in the lobby waiting for you."

The ice that had filled my veins crystallized.

Minnie ... I'd let Minnie down. How the heck would I face her?

MINNIE LOOKED up from her magazine as the door of the principal's office closed behind me. Her brow furrowed in concern and she stood quickly.

"Are you okay?"

Was *I* okay? "Are you serious? You're worried about *me*?"

Her frown deepened. "You stabbed yourself in the heart, Indie. Yeah, I'm worried. You were gone from sim class before we could exit the sim, and then Garnet tells me you were summoned to the principal's office ... I didn't know what to think."

"I just cost you the exam."

Minnie reached for my hands. "I don't give a shit about that right now. I'm worried about you. I need to know you're okay."

Something bubbled up inside me. A welling feeling I'd kept at bay for the longest time. It expanded to fill my chest, rose up my throat, and pressed the back of my eyes and nose with a familiar sting.

And then my vision blurred. No. Fuck no.

"Indie? Oh, shit. Indie." Minnie pulled me into a hug, and a strangled sob broke from my throat.

"Shit." My voice sounded odd. I cleared my throat. "I'm fine."

I pulled away, and she let me go, but the look in her eyes was determined. "No. Not this time. We need to talk. You need to tell me what happened, not just in the sim, but before you came here. It's eating away at you. I know it is."

The fight bled out of me. Maybe she was right. Maybe it was time to offload.

"Not here. Let's go back to the dorm."

ONCE I STARTED TALKING about that night, about the loss of control and the blackout, the words poured out. My father's face swam in my mind's eye, cold and uncaring. His voice matter-of-fact as he laid out the terms. He'd done this to me. He'd somehow orchestrated my crime and was now forcing me into a role that would never fit.

"I don't understand why." I picked at the edge of the throw on my bed. "He hates me."

"That can't be true ..." But she didn't sound too sure.

I looked up at her with a wry smile. "My father has been very vocal about his desire for a son. I doubt anyone in the legacy circles could have missed that."

She winced. "Yeah, it may have come up now and then."

"Unfortunately, my mother never conceived again. I'm all he has, a reminder of what he considers his failure, and my father does not like to fail. He's the first Justice not to produce a male heir."

"Oh, babe." Minnie sat cross-legged on the rug between our beds. "And then you had the bloodlust come over you—your worst fear … No wonder you bailed."

"And now you failed the class." I swallowed the lump on my throat. "I'm sorry."

"Don't be. So, my A minus drops to a B." She flashed her teeth in a cheeky grin. "I'll make it up."

She was covering. Faradays were renowned for the pressure they put on their offspring to succeed. A B average would not be enough.

Her expression sobered. "But what about you? I caught something about grades?"

Nightblood hearing had its perks. "If I don't maintain a C grade or above, then I'm toast."

We sat in silence for a long minute.

"You'll keep the grade," Minnie said. "We'll cram for the end-of-term tests, and we'll both ace them." Her eyes lit up. "Indie. You can do this. You know you can."

The confidence in her tone was infectious. I was far from dumb, I just preferred not to work at the academics. But with my head on the line, there was no choice but to employ the brain cells.

"We'll get to work right after the goblet ceremony tomorrow." Minnie got up and hurried to her wardrobe. "In the meantime, we're going to get dressed and go to a party."

"Urgh." I slumped back on the bed. "I am in no mood to party."

She threw some silken fabric at my face. "Put that on. I won't take no for an answer."

"Nothing new there." But I couldn't keep the smile out of my voice.

The fabric was a cerulean halter-neck top. Sod it. After the shitty day, and the shitty news, maybe a party was just what the doctor ordered.

THE PARTY WAS in a clearing in the forest behind the Academy that everyone had dubbed "the grove." The cadets of the Academy had used the grove for generations, and even though the gatherings weren't authorized by administration, everyone knew they turned a blind eye to the merrymaking.

We slipped out from the hulking shadow of the Academy building and joined the train of students dressed in jeans, flats, T-shirts, and fancy tops heading into the forest. I'd opted for sneakers, dark jeans, and the cerulean halter neck Minnie had lobbed at me. I'd pulled my hair back into a French braid, added a lick of gloss and a dash of mascara—my tribute to makeup.

Minnie looked hot in skinny jeans, ballet flats, and smoky eye makeup that brought out the emerald in her eyes.

My gray eyes were unremarkable in comparison.

Heck, I'd never relied on my looks, though; my smart mouth was what got me places.

And here we were, slipping under the canopy of trees into the cool confines of the forest. The aromas of earth and flora filled my head, and then we were running, weaving through the trees toward the grove. Howls rose up on either side of us. Wolves on a run. Free, wild, and natural. The nightblood beneath my skin surged to the surface, and with a challenging glance Minnie's way, I broke into fast mode.

The world whizzed by with the scrape of leaves, the slash of branches, and the exhilaration of the chase. Minnie was on my tail. She was fast, but heck, I was faster.

I leapt over a log and landed on the edge of the grove. The sounds of the party wrapped themselves around me—music, laughter, and the distinct aroma of poppy seed cigarettes, a favorite of the feyblood.

Minnie joined me a moment later. "Damn, Indie. You're rocket-powered."

"Yeah, shoved one up my butt before we left the dorm."

"Don't look now, but Thomas is heading over." She moved closer to me. "If he mentions the damned test, I'll nut him."

Thomas stopped a few feet away from us, hands in his pockets. "You okay?" he mumbled.

Wait, what? Had I just heard right? "Who are you,

77

and what have you done with the intolerant nightblood called Thomas?"

He gave me a smile and opened his mouth to say something.

"Hey, Carmichael, you gone over to the dark side now?" someone called out.

I looked over his shoulder to see a group of nightbloods holding drinks. Carmichael and Hartwood lads.

"Nah!" Thomas backed away from us as if we gave off toxic fumes. "Just checking out the freak show."

I shook my head. "And there he is."

Minnie snorted. "Sheep." She linked arms with me. "Come on, let's get a drink."

Alcohol didn't affect supernaturals the same way it did humans, but it did give us a warm buzz. It made the world a little softer. A trestle table had been set up to one side, and we wove our way toward it, past half-naked grinding moonkissed and necking nightbloods. Past feybloods in lip locks and toward sanctuary.

How many of the guys here would be with us tomorrow, and how many will have been shadow marked and shipped off to the shadow cadet wing?

"Shit, these things get steamy," Minnie said as we reached the table.

Several bottles of lethally strong vodka were lined up on it with neat piles of plastic cups.

I grabbed a cup and filled it. "Horny supernaturals on a full moon."

"And bitchy supernaturals on the prowl," Minnie said. "Harper alert."

Oh, great. I turned to find Harper and her posse descending on us. Tonight they were dressed in various shades of green. They looked good, and plenty of male heads swiveled their way, but Harper had eyes only for Minnie. She stopped a little way away and said something to her girls. They turned and melted into the crowd as she approached us.

"Hey, Min, you look good," she said. "I was hoping we could talk." Her gaze slid to me then back to Minnie. "Alone."

Minnie tensed. "If you're here to apologize for the way you spoke to Indie then I'm happy to chat. If not, then we have nothing to talk about."

Harper crossed her arms, and for a moment, there was a look of vulnerability on her overly painted face. She glanced over her shoulder to where her posse was mingling and then fixed her eyes on me.

"Look, I'm sorry if I offended you. But you know what I said was true. You *are* a criminal. You're here because you have to be, not because you want to be. You don't even care about being in the Nightwatch."

Her words, which would have been like water off a duck's back a day ago, hit home hard. She was right. All of it, and in that moment, I saw myself through her eyes—an uncaring, snarky woman who'd come in and stolen her friend.

"Harper!" Minnie chided.

Harper held up her hands. "I'm trying here, Min. Just ... Can we please go for a walk and chat?"

Minnie shook her head, but I caught the hesitation. She and Harper had been close before me. She had to have seen something in the blonde bombshell to be friends with her.

"Go." I shrugged. "If I'm going to be taking this Academy stuff seriously, I should probably try and mingle."

Harper looked at me in surprise.

Minnie locked gazes with me. "You're just going to stand here and drink, aren't you?"

I downed the contents of my cup and poured another. "Pretty much. But it makes me happy." I raised my cup.

Minnie narrowed her eyes. "I'll be right back. Hide a bottle for me."

She headed off with Harper, and they slipped into the forest.

My stomach quivered. Fuck, this friendship shit was dangerous. It had you caring and feeling insecure and—

"What the fuck?" Harmon's gruff voice, raised in anger, cut across the clearing.

I tracked the commotion to several half naked moonkissed being herded into the clearing by a group of guys dressed in black. Booted and lethal-looking, they caused the volume in the clearing to drop instantly and drew every eye.

Shadow cadets.

Second years by the looks of the burgundy emblems on their shirts. Hair combed back and clean shaven, they were the epitome of what the shadow knights were all about, and in a year, they'd be joining the veterans at the fortress.

Shadow cadet training was super strict. Fun was prohibited, or so I'd gleaned in my time here. The shadow cadets didn't join in the social events of the Nightwatch Academy, so what were they doing here tonight?

Harmon thrust out his hairy chest and advanced on one of the cadets, who placed a hand on his shoulder and brought him to his knees. A petite, dark-haired moonkissed girl ran forward, yelling at the shadow cadet to let her brother go.

Lottie Black. Spitfire extraordinaire. She had a temper as volatile as mine but none of the control. So far, we hadn't shared any classes.

The cadet shoved her away, his face contorted in anger, but he did release Harmon, who glared up at him murderously. Lottie fell to her knees by her brother, and murmurs broke out across the clearing. Angry and shocked.

What the hell?

The shadow cadets fanned out, circling the grove. Wait, was that a glint of steel at their sides. Weapons? They had weapons. What the fuck?

Something was wrong, and the atmosphere was now one of tension.

A familiar blond head came into view. Piercing blue eyes cast a net over the grove, and a chiseled jaw flexed with intensity. Lloyd Faraday stood at the edge of the clearing several meters away and proceeded to scan the crowd.

Minnie's brother was there. This visit had to be official because no way would the stick-in-the-mud break protocol for a party. So, the question remained, what was he doing there?

The last thing I wanted was to be in Lloyd Faraday's orbit. Derision didn't look good spattered all over me, but my curiosity was piqued. Throwing back the drink in my hand, I headed across the clearing toward him.

Lloyd's attention zeroed in on me as I approached. His nostrils flared in annoyance.

I crossed my arms, needing some defense against his searing gaze. "What the hell is going on?"

His attention slipped over my shoulder and then back again. "Nothing for you to worry about. Just remain in the clearing. Do not try and leave." He made to brush past me, but I grabbed his arm.

I could smell his anxiety and hear the rise in his pulse. "You're ... afraid."

His gaze slashed across my face. "I am not afraid. I'm concerned. You shouldn't be out here. This is an unauthorized gathering. But then that's typical of a rule breaker like you, isn't it?"

"Look around, arsehole. I'm not the only one here. This shindig happens every term, and no one bats an eye, yet here you cadets are, surrounding the grove while carrying weapons." My pulse spiked. Wait a minute. They were here as protection. They were here as a guard. "What is it? What are you protecting us from?"

My gaze flicked to the left where a feyblood couple was blocked from wandering off into the forest by one of the cadets. The feyblood looked familiar, and then I caught sight of his profile. Oberon. Figured.

He was squaring off with the cadet now, getting irate.

Lloyd pulled out of my grip, but I stepped into his path.

"You're supposed to keep us here, aren't you?" I peered up at his stern face. "Is there something out there?" My pulse kicked up as the scenario suddenly made sense. "Lloyd, for fucksake answer me. Is there something out there?"

He took a sharp breath through his nose. "Just stay put, and everything will be fine. We have it covered. Everyone is either right here or back at the Academy."

My breath was coming shallow. "No. No, they're not."

His eyes widened. "Minnie's not back at the Academy, is she?"

I shook my head slowly.

And then a female scream cut across the grove.

NINE

Minnie was in danger.

Nothing else mattered.

There was no stopping me as I blurred past Lloyd and into the forest.

Another scream.

Over fallen tree trunks, and through tangled branches.

Two figures came into view. Back to back with a silvery orb surrounding them.

I skidded to a halt, kicking up dirt.

Harper's feyblood protection was shielding them from something. But what? I scanned the clearing for the threat.

"Indie, watch out!" Minnie warned.

Something flesh-colored and huge slammed into me from the side, taking me down. My breath whooshed out of my lungs, and a crack was followed by darkness and stars.

Shit.

Do not pass out.

Adrenaline surged through my limbs as my nightblood power took over, and my arms shot up to ward off the beast. Red eyes burned into me from either side of a wide snout with bumpy ridges running up it. A fomorian hound. I'd seen pictures, but how the heck was it here?

Jaws snapped in my face, drool splashed my cheek. My head began to tingle, and my vision blurred.

What the fuck, what the—I bunched my muscles and put everything into the release of tension, throwing the creature off. It slid across the earth, and then snapped its head back toward me and charged again. I braced, ready for impact, but the monster never made it to me. It was met by a mass of muscle and power dressed in black and blue.

Archer Hyde's six-foot-six frame of muscle grappled with the hound, forcing it back, forcing it away from me. The hound resisted, but Archer locked down. Unmoving, unyielding.

His bionic leg. It was giving him the upper hand. I raked my gaze down his powerful back, over his taut buttocks, and skimmed his legs. The material of the cargo pants was too baggy to make out which leg was the real one and which was the mech one.

"My sword!" he called out over his shoulder.

It was strapped to his back. He couldn't get to it, not without releasing the hound.

I broke into a run toward him at the same time as Lloyd exploded into the clearing along with two other cadets. They cut across me and made a beeline for Archer and the hound. There was a loud snapping sound.

"Stop!"

A barrel-chested, bearded man huffed into the clearing followed by a woman dressed in a dark cloak. He was clutching a sword that seemed like a little bit of an overcompensation, if you get what I mean.

"Don't hurt it," beard guy shouted. "I can wrangle it."

But the beast lay still, its neck at an odd angle.

Archer stepped away from the hound. "Too late for wrangling. Any more escapees we need to know about?" he snarled. "You have one job, Redmond. One. You almost got these cadets killed." His gaze flicked to me briefly before returning to Redmond. "Are there any more?"

Redmond looked over at the cloaked woman, then to the fallen hound. He shook his head and stood taller. "No. We *caught* the other youngling, which is what we asked you for help with. Catching, not killing." He sounded pissed.

Hyde's expression was unreadable. "My priority is the cadets at this Academy."

"You used to care about these beasts once," Redmond threw back.

"But now they're your problem," Hyde said.

"We should get back." The woman's voice was smooth and calm. Something glinted green on her chest. An amulet? The mark of an official weaver. "We need to check the warding and dispose of the dead."

"You need to report to Brunner," Archer said. "She should know about this breach."

Redmond held up his hands. "Wait a second, Archer. I came to you for help because of your expertise at wrangling these hounds. You know me. You know I don't make mistakes. This is hardly a breach. A few younglings escaped their pens before I could get them into the catacombs. We dealt with it, so why bother the administration?"

Archer crossed his arms and glared at Redmond.

"You owe me, Hyde."

Archer's shoulders relaxed. "Damn you. If this happens again ..."

"It won't. Mariana and I will get the body back to the stables. Thank you for your assistance."

Archer made a sound of disgust deep in his throat and turned his attention to me. He strode over, and then his impressive frame and his lethal aura were pressing in on me, surrounding me so it was hard to draw breath.

He stopped a foot away, forcing me to crane my neck to look up into his scarred face. That close, it was easier to see his Tuatha ancestry. The hard, chiseled features, the pout of his mouth, the slightly flared nostrils, and thick dark lashes. He had been beautiful once, was still beautiful beneath the scars that slanted diagonally across his face. His eyes were what captivated me, though. A color somewhere between blue and green were hard with anger.

He looked down his nose at me. "You're lucky to be alive, cadet."

His tone was low and abrasive to my senses, but in a way that sent shivers of desire down my spine. Shitting heck. I took a step away from him but not before I caught a whiff of his citrus aroma and the sweet scent of blood rushing beneath. A sound somewhere between a groan and a moan escaped my lips. I clamped my mouth shut and stared up at him, mortified.

He arched a brow and then his lip curled slightly. "You got lucky. Next time you see a huge fucking fomorian hound, run." He turned away and strode toward the tree line. "Get back to the dorm," he called out as he vanished between the trees.

The two cadets with Lloyd said something to him, then jogged off after Archer. Lloyd headed toward Minnie.

Harper's silver shield had vanished, and Minnie ran into her brother's arms.

"Damn it, Minnie," Lloyd snapped. "Fucking hell. I thought ... Oh, God."

They hugged tight, and my gaze went to Harper, whose eyes were dazed and fixed on her friend.

My friend.

But if not for that shield …

Everyone knew how Bourne feyblood powers worked. They were more Tuatha than lower fey, and they had something called the shining—a defensive halo that enveloped them in protection when they were in mortal danger. It came in very useful as a Nightwatch agent. But what many people didn't know, and what I knew – due to my time in the slums with all its dirty secrets—was that the shining could only be extended to protect a loved one.

Loved one.

Harper loved Minnie, and from the look on her face a moment ago, it wasn't in a platonic way. It was obvious Minnie had no clue. The jealousy and prejudice I'd thought had prompted Harper's bitchiness toward me was much more than that. It was pain.

I walked over to Harper. "Good thinking on the shield."

Her expression closed, and she shrugged and hugged herself. "It was instinct."

Minnie wrapped her arms around me and squeezed. "Crazy bitch, you could have been killed."

I hugged her back, and Harper averted her gaze.

Minnie released me. "Come on. Lloyd's going to walk us back to the Academy."

I looked over to find Lloyd staring right at me, his mouth pressed in a thin line like he was holding back a tide of words. Critical ones, no doubt.

Yeah, keep them to yourself, blondie.

It was only when we were exiting the clearing that I realized that I hadn't noticed Redmond and the weaver leave with the youngling.

TEN

B ack in the confines of our dorm room, the events of the night seemed like a bad dream. We'd been attacked by a fomorian hound. A youngling, but still. If Harper hadn't acted so quick, if she wasn't in love with Minnie, then Minnie would be dead.

I glanced over at my friend from my bed. Just the top of her head peeked out from the covers. It wasn't my place to tell her. Not my place to reveal someone else's heart.

Or maybe you just don't want to lose your only friend.

Piss off, inner voice of reason.

"What the hell were fomorian hounds doing on Academy grounds?" Minnie said softly, breaking the silence.

Ah, so she'd emerged from her cocoon.

"Wreaking havoc. We were lucky no one was seriously hurt." I pulled the covers over me and snuggled down under them. "Who's that Redmond guy?"

"He's the shadow trial master," Minnie said. "He's responsible for catching fomorian hounds that come into the mist. Not sure what he does with them, probably tames them ... I'm not sure."

"What's a shadow trial?"

"The test that shadow cadets take. Not sure what it involves, though. Lloyd wouldn't go into detail. I don't think they're supposed to talk about them. I don't even think he should have told me about the hounds they keep stabled at the fortress."

So much for no threat around the Academy. "And the weaver. I haven't seen her about."

"And you wouldn't. Mariana Latrou works at the fortress now. She used to teach Defense Against Weaving. But Master Payne took over the class, and she was ... promoted, I guess?" Minnie was silent for a long time. "You know, this makes no sense. That was a youngling. Younglings born on this side of the mist are tame, at least they're supposed to be. I know the knights use hounds raised here against the hounds born on the other side when they patrol the mist."

"So? This one wasn't trained properly. They're beasts. Otherworld beasts."

"But there was more than one out there. Seems odd to have two or three untrainable younglings in one batch ..."

"Do you train younglings often?"

She laughed. "Point taken. Thank God Master Hyde showed up."

"Yeah, I doubt Archer would have let Redmond off the hook about Brunner if the youngling thing was a huge issue."

"Archer, is it?" There was a smile in Minnie's voice. "I knew he'd catch your eye. The dangerous-looking ex-shadow knight. But I doubt he'd appreciate you calling him by his first name, not that you'll ever have reason to call him anything. We won't be working with him. He trains the shadow cadets. Also, technically, Redmond outranks Hyde. I heard that Hyde used to be Trial Master before Redmond. It's a position that comes with some major perks, so Hyde had it good. I guess if you're going to go into the mist and catch wild hounds, then you deserve extra benefits. Didn't work out too great for Hyde, though. They say it's how he lost his leg. Anyway, once he was injured, Redmond was given Hyde's job."

Master Hyde ... Archer Hyde. There was something about him. A pull, a presence. My body tightened at the memory of his proximity. I blew out a harsh breath. It had obviously been too long since I'd had sex.

I rolled onto my front and tucked my arms under the pillow in my comfy position. "He took that youngling on single-handed. Just held its jaws open with his bare hands."

"What about you? I thought it was going to bite

your head off, and then you kicked it across the clearing."

Yeah ... Yeah. I had. Thinking back on it ... How the fuck had I done that?

"Get some sleep," Minnie said. "We hit the books hard once the goblet ceremony is over."

"THIS IS THE LIBRARY." Minnie swept through the huge double doors and did a cute little wave thing as if introducing me to an actual person. "Library, this is Justice, she will be nestling in your bosom soon."

I shook my head and laughed softly. "I don't nestle."

But there was no denying the room had allure. Moonlight streamed in from tall, thin gothic windows but was overshadowed by the lights from two huge chandeliers hanging high above us.

The ceiling was a floor high, and balconies ran along the periphery of the room, but both floors were home to sofas and desks, not books. In fact, the only floor with any books was the one we were standing on. They filled a wall to our left and several stacks in the center of the room. Students sat at long tables, heads down, studying. Others sat on comfy sofas arranged in clusters with coffee mugs and fiction novels. A warm hush filled the room, the hush of knowledge being absorbed and worlds being explored.

Minnie leaned in. "Reference books to the left. Most of the stacks contain plastic slip-covered articles and accounts of attacks and supernatural events that have occurred over the last few centuries. We have a ton of history books to help us study the evolution of man. We also have a cool fiction section, mainly contemporary romance and literary fiction. I mean, who wants to read fantasy when you're living it, although we do have a few novels that are on the required texts for Supernaturals in Human Society classes." She led the way through the stacks. "It helps to blend in and to understand the human psyche if we look at what's prominent in fantasy literature."

It was cool and silent in the stacks, like a different world. The shelves rose high on either side of us, and even though the ceiling was a floor above us, there was still a sense of being cocooned.

"You'd be surprised how many books *haven't* been written on the supernatural and the mist," Minnie said. "The ones that matter are kept at headquarters. But we have what we need, and at the Academy, the tutors are the real books."

I stared at her. "That was kind of poetic."

Her cheeks flushed. "I suppose it was." She took a left, and there was a cluster of sofas, a coffee table, and a desk for two. "This is our spot." She smiled. "I like to come here to study. It's been a Faraday haunt forever. Lloyd left it to me."

"You can't just leave someone a spot in a library."

She snorted. "Have you met my family?"

"Point taken."

"This will be our hangout as of tomorrow. Come on, we better get to class."

MADAM GARNET, the sim tutor, also taught Endangered Supernatural Species in a small room on the first floor of the study wing. It was cramped, but the class was small because it wasn't a required class, but an elective, one my father had thought it prudent to have added to my schedule.

It was also our last class for the evening. With the goblet ceremony ball pending, the scholastic day had been cut short.

But even though the room buzzed with excitement and anticipation for the festivities to come, there was no tuning out in Garnet's class, plus, since I needed to keep my grade up, I'd better pay attention.

A couple of months ago, my only worries were which fights to pick, and how to make enough money to avoid having to dip into the fund daddy had set up for me. And now I was wearing an actual uniform and sitting in class, paying attention like a good little student.

It made me sick.

Because this wasn't me. It was another attempt by Daddy Dearest to make me into the person he wanted me to be. The person I'd given up trying to be months ago.

I wasn't a student or a scholar. I led with my fists and lived on instinct, not logic. But this was survival. Pass and live, or fail and die. Simple. Once this was over, we'd be given a choice—take up the Nightwatch mantle or decline. I could walk away having kept my part of the deal, because nothing in the deal said I had to actually be a Watch agent, just that I had to come to the Academy and graduate.

"Miss Justice!" Garnet's voice snapped me out of my reverie. "Morphs. Go."

Morphs? What the ... I looked to Minnie in a panic.

Garnet rolled her eyes. "Points for attending, Miss Justice, but you won't get the grades if you don't bloody pay attention. Miss Faraday, how about you educate your friend."

Minnie shot me a sheepish look. "A morph is a creature that can take the form of any other living thing as long as that living thing has just died."

"Correct." Miss Garnet perched on the edge of her desk, booted legs crossed. "Morphs have been hunted for generations, considered dangerous because of their ability to take on not just someone's form but also their memories. The council has issued a law to protect the species, but it's been several decades since a morph has been seen."

"And how would you know even if you did see

one?" Harmon asked from the back of the class. "I mean if they can take on any form."

Garnet grinned. "I guess you wouldn't." She clapped her hands. "Next up, the Impox. Who can tell me about those?" She scanned the class. "Mr. Carmichael?"

Thomas lounged in a seat by the window, his long legs stretched out under the table. "Fox spirit and imp hybrids. Feybloods renowned for their ability to control the minds of others once they've tasted their blood."

Urgh. I was beginning to sense a theme with the whole endangered thing. Mind manipulation, shape shifting, it was like the Watch strived to eliminate any threat to the status quo.

"Aren't they extinct?" someone else asked.

"Not quite," Garnet said. "We have a few in captivity." She stood and rounded her desk and flipped through a huge book. "You'll be tested on endangered creatures at the end of the term. I suggest you all brush up on them." Her gaze fell on me. "I'm always here if you need help." She stood tall and glared at us. "Now, get your arses out of here, and get ready for the ceremony."

A collective whoop went up, chairs scraped as one, and bodies headed for the door.

The weight of how much I didn't know would have to wait. I had a party to go to.

MINNIE SMOOTHED down her uniform and fiddled with her hair, which was perfect as usual. Her side of the room looked like a bomb had hit it, which was strange considering the dress code was uniforms.

I tugged at the neck of my tunic. "Why do they have to make these things so uncomfortable?"

"It's only because you haven't bothered with a uniform since you got here," Minnie said. "You'll get used to it."

"It's a fucking party, and we have to wear this shit?"

"It's a ceremony."

"With food and booze, right?"

"Not booze." She turned to me with a shocked expression. "The revelation nectar. Seriously, Indie, how do you not know this stuff?"

"Because it's the kind of stuff you learn from your parents, and mine had no interest in teaching me." I turned away and grabbed a hair brush off my dresser. "I wasn't worth the effort."

"Indie ..."

I shot her a wry smile. "It's fine. I'm not feeling sorry for myself. It's just a fact. They wanted a son to carry on the Justice name for our line—sons mean a larger cut of the pie when it comes to inheritances and legacy money. But they got me instead." I began to brush my hair. Why was I telling her this stuff? I never talked about this shit. But the words were pouring out now. "I was five when I heard them talking about it. I'd just learned to tie my shoelaces, and I ran to their chambers to tell them. I heard them talking about me. My mother said they'd need to make the best of it, and my father was adamant they should keep trying for a son. I had toys and clothes and a pretty room, but I didn't have their love, and suddenly, it made sense why. They wanted a boy." I began to braid my hair. "So, I decided to become one. I put away the pretty dolls and picked up a rapier. I learned to fence and box. I got into sports and athletics. But nothing mattered. It took me a while to figure out the whole money thing, the legacy inheritance, and the way it was determined by male bloodlines. I knew then they'd never love me the way parents are supposed to. So, I left."

"Indie, I'm so sorry." Minnie stroked my arm. "That's harsh."

"It's life, and I'm over it. Once I finish my sentence here, I'm out. Like hell am I dancing to anyone else's tune ever again."

She blinked up at me. "But you won't forget me, will you?"

My heart squeezed painfully in my chest. Should I tell her she was my first real friend? The first person not paid or coerced to spend time with me? Should I tell her that she was the only person that made this place bearable?"

"No, Min, I don't think I could ever forget you."

She grinned. "Good, because if you try and do a

vanishing act on me, I will have no problem using my Nightwatch skills to hunt you down."

I didn't doubt her.

She tucked her hair behind her ears and pouted at herself in the mirror. "Now, let's go watch some shadow cadets be crowned. I hear they have seven different kinds of cake at these things."

Despite my general derision and disinterest in everything Academy, there was a definite pique in my curiosity. Not many people could say they got to experience a Revelation ceremony. And they had cake.

It might be fun ... right?

ELEVEN

There was a general aura of high expectation on the air, especially among the males. After all, the shadow knight gene was passed down from male to male. How many cadets would be identified tonight? How many would be marked once they drank the revelation nectar?

Cadets swept down the main staircase into the huge foyer that was lit up like it was winter solstice. Usually, the Academy conserved energy—after all, we all had excellent night vision and senses here—but not tonight. Tonight, they'd gone all out to make the place shine. We turned left at the bottom of the staircase, away from the study wing and into the main section of the Academy—one opened up only on special occasions. This was the hub portion of the structure where all the main events and ceremonies were held. And tonight was the first huge ceremony of the year.

Identification of the next batch of shadow knights.

And boy, did the guys look happy with the thought of being marked for death.

Idiots.

A glimpse through the huge double doors that had been pulled back showed a vast room with high, vaulted ceilings and huge gothic paned windows decorated in the classic fleur-de-lis design.

Round tables had been set up, each fit to seat eight, but this wasn't a sit-where-you-please affair, there was a table plan parked outside the room. A crowd had gathered around it, and Minnie craned her neck to check it out.

We pushed into the excited buzz of voices, trying to get closer to the plan. We were almost at the front when the hubbub dulled and the foyer fell into almost silence. Minnie grabbed my arm and tugged me back slightly.

"What?"

The scent of jasmine and roses hit me in the face, and then a group of cadets dressed in eveningwear swept past us and right to the front of the crowd. I caught a glimpse of silk and the tailored back of a dress coat.

"What the heck?"

Minnie sighed. "Weavers. They think they're better than everyone else just because they can manipulate the arcana in the air." She shook her head. "Or turn us into toads."

The weavers were the linchpin of the Nightwatch. The whole system would fall apart without their abilities. I bit my tongue and watched as a chestnut-haired beauty with startling gray-blue eyes studied the chart. She dimpled at her escort and then swept away from us and toward the ceremony hall.

"Fiona Payne is sooo hot," someone behind me muttered.

Payne, like Master Payne. There were only three weaver families—Latrou, Raj, and Payne—and they were a close-knit community that kept to themselves. The weavers even had their own wing here, and separate lessons entirely. I don't think I'd ever seen one in the dining hall. I turned to Minnie to ask her where the weavers ate.

"Table three," Minnie said. "Urgh. Thomas, Harmon, and Oberon are with us." She pursed her lips. "Harper, Lottie, and someone called Nettie."

My questions could wait. "Well, let's get in there."

The smell of roasting meat was strong on the air. The moonkissed were probably salivating. Bowls overflowing with fruit lined the side of the room, and in the center of each table was a huge golden goblet embedded with rubies. The precious stones winked like drops of blood.

My stomach rumbled.

Minnie wove her way between the tables, cutting a path through the other cadets. Our table was halfway across the room and left of center.

Minnie pulled out a chair and sat down. "You're next to me."

I took a seat, relieved to no longer be part of the throng. A door at the back of the room opened, and the tutors began to file in. Garnet, Master Payne, and Master Decker, followed by several faces I didn't recognize. They took seats at a long table that faced the room. Brunner came next, followed by the bearded dude—Redmond—and finally, Archer Hyde. Tonight, he was dressed in a form-fitting black shirt and gray cargo pants; ink peeked from beneath the collar of his shirt and curled up around his neck. How had I missed that? In profile, his scars weren't as evident, but the cut of his jaw and the sharp line of his aquiline nose were. The shorn hair just made him look more dangerous.

"Um, Indie, you're staring," Minnie said.

Shit. The guy was a veteran shadow knight— probably late twenties—seasoned and too old for me. Plus, he was a tutor for God's sake. I needed to get my shit together.

But the air of danger that cloaked him was an aphrodisiac that called to me. It was fists and daggers and freedom. It was sexual heat and want. The pulse at my throat fluttered at the thought of being close to him, of inhaling that citrus scent again.

I needed to get laid. Bad.

"Lady and not so lady." Thomas took a seat opposite us.

Harmon joined us a moment later. He looked on

edge. "Fuck, I wish they'd just get it over with. All the pomp and shit. Unnecessary."

Thomas's jaw ticked. "We talked about this. It's tradition."

Harper appeared to Minnie's left. "Excited?" She took her seat.

Minnie laughed. "For the cake, yes."

"Yeah, you guys have nothing to worry about," Harmon said. "Not like you're about to get the death stamp."

I locked gazes with him, shocked.

"What?" His lip curled.

I shrugged. "Nothing. Just thought I was the only one who thought of it that way."

Harmon snorted. "Well, you're not. Trust me, I'm not the only one who feels that way. Did you know that they send moonkissed shadow knights into the mist first? They use them like fucking hounds."

"That's a vile rumor," Thomas snapped. "The Watch would never do that."

"Oh, and you know this because you happen to come from a legacy family? Well, moonkissed aren't part of the legacy posse, we only get a cursory place on the council."

Thomas's face fell. "I'm sorry you feel that way, but the system works."

"Does it?" Harmon glared at Thomas.

I looked to Minnie, who was sharing a wince with Harper.

Fuck this. "Hey, drop it. Both of you. It is what it is. We can't change it. And if you get picked, you don't have to accept the position as shadow cadet. You can decline."

All eyes were suddenly on me.

Harmon let out a bark of laughter and shook his head. "You really have been out of the loop, haven't you? Not that it affects you, but the law changed last year. If you're marked, then it counts as conscription. There is no way out. You try and leave, and they will execute you for treason to the council."

What the fuck? "They can't do that."

"They can, and they have," Minnie said softly. "It seems that the number of shadow knights being born is dropping. There's even talk of making the nectar compulsory to every supernatural male over the age of sixteen."

Harper continued. "But the opposition from the legacy families is all that's keeping that law from being passed right now. However, if the number of shadow cadets falls any further, then it might become a reality."

Oberon approached the table, his golden hair pulled back off a face that was paler than usual.

"Let's get this over with," he muttered.

A bell rang just as the last people at our table joined us. A stocky, angry-looking feyblood sat to my right. She shot me a glare before fixing her attention on the tutor table. This had to be Nettie.

Harmon looked to the doorway, probably to see if Lottie was about, but then Principal Brunner was speaking.

"Welcome to the Revelation ceremony, cadets. Tonight, we will unveil our next class of shadow cadets, and we will celebrate the continued protection of our world." She reached for the goblet before her. "Please, stand."

The room was filled with the sound of chair legs scraping against polished wood.

"The goblet before you is filled with revelation nectar. You will each take a sip, male or female, as we are united in this revelation that protects us all."

Hyde stepped off the raised platform housing the tutors' table and onto the main floor.

Around us, cadets began to drink. Thomas took a deep breath and reached for the goblet, but Harmon got to it first.

He raised it in a mock salute. "Fuck it." He took a swig and passed it to Thomas.

The nightblood took a sip, and then Harper took a gulp.

"Yum." She passed it to Minnie.

Minnie took a dainty sip and held it out to me. "Tastes good."

I took the huge goblet and sniffed. It didn't smell of anything. I shrugged and took a sip. Flavor exploded on my tongue as the cool liquid slid down my throat. It was sweet and tangy at the same time.

Nice.

I handed the goblet to Nettie, who swigged and handed it to Oberon.

"Fuck!" Harmon grabbed his forearm and shoved his sleeve up to reveal a crescent-shaped mark with a line through it. "Oh, shit."

Thomas looked up at his lover in shock. "Harmon … I'm so—Ouch." He grabbed the back of his hand, his eyes wide.

"Show me," Harmon said.

Thomas revealed the back of his palm, which had an identical mark to Harmon's on it.

They could both be arseholes, but they didn't deserve conscription. My heart sank on their behalf.

Around us, more and more exclamations filled the air. Most were celebratory. I guessed not everyone understood what being a shadow knight would entail, or maybe they did and were just uber brave, like the man who was weaving in between the tables, taking a mental note of all those exhibiting a mark.

Oberon cursed softly.

"You too?" Thomas asked him.

He shook his head. "No. I … I don't feel anything." His eyes widened in panic. "What the fuck?"

"You're lucky," Harmon sneered. "You get to live."

"It'll be over soon." Minnie smiled. "Then we get to eat cake. Lloyd said last year they had warm blood as if it had just been tapped from the vein."

My stomach grumbled again. I needed blood. I

squeezed my eyes shut. It would be fine. It was bagged, so it was fine.

Heat bloomed across my collarbones and then coalesced at a single point above my right breast in an intense burning sensation.

"Fucking hell." I slapped a hand over the spot and rubbed it through the material of my tunic.

"You okay?" Minnie reached for my collar.

"I think something bit me." I tugged at my tunic, wanting to get at the offending insect and stop the pain. There was a slight rip, and then the material was loose enough to look down.

There was something there. Something black. Unmoving. Ice filled my veins.

Not an insect.

"Indie?" Minnie leaned in and peered down my top. Her head whipped up so fast she almost smacked me in the chin. Her face drained of color. "No ..."

A shadow fell over us.

"What's going on?" Archer Hyde asked.

Minnie stepped back, her mouth parted in shock.

I looked up at Master Hyde, my pulse pounding in my throat like a tribal drum. "I don't understand."

I pulled down the top to reveal the mark that now marred my skin.

He reached out to graze it with his fingers, searing me with a new kind of heat and sending my pulse galloping.

"What is it?" My voice was a breathless whisper.

He locked gazes with me, his green-blue eyes boring into my soul. "It's the mark. The mark of a shadow knight."

TWELVE

Brunner stared at me from behind her desk, her face an unreadable mask. They'd placed a chair against the wall, so I was facing the room as a whole. Master Hyde leaned up against the windowsill, his arms crossed over his chest. Madam Garnet had taken up a spot by the bookcase opposite me, and now they were all staring at me.

So much for getting to eat cake.

Hyde had dragged me out of the ballroom so fast my head had spun. We'd come straight here, and the last six minutes had passed in silence. It didn't look like anyone was going to be breaking that silence any time soon.

There was a mark on my chest. A shadow mark.

It had to be a mistake.

There was no other answer.

The door opened, and a portly man with wispy gray hair and ruddy cheeks stumbled in.

His attention went straight to Brunner. "Ines, you wished to ... Oh, ah, hello there, Archer. Melle." He nodded at Garnet. His gaze fell on me. "Student whose name I do not know." He smiled pleasantly before focusing on the principal again. "You wanted to see me?"

Brunner tapped her fingers on the desk. "The revelation nectar ..."

"Yes?"

"You mixed it to the usual specifications?"

He frowned. "Um, yes. Yes, of course I did. Is there a problem?"

Brunner fixed her steely eyes on me. "Master Herman is responsible for our hothouse and also takes Herbs and Toxins. Show him please, Miss Justice."

I tugged my top down to show yet another person the top of my tit.

His hand flew to his mouth, and his ruddy cheeks lost the red tinge. "Oh ... Oh, my." His hands fluttered around his face. "Two parts honey pea, three parts Linga root ..." He fell into a mutter, reciting the secret recipe. He looked up and nodded. "Perfect. It was perfect. You have others marked? Males?"

Brunner nodded.

"Then it works. The nectar works as it always has."

Hyde pushed off the sill, and his arms dropped to his sides. "But she's a fucking woman."

"Ten out of ten for observation." The words were out before I could stop them.

He glared at me, and I glared back. Like hell would I be cowed, no matter how badly my limbs were quivering right now.

I looked to Brunner. "It's obviously a mistake. Shadow knights are male." I indicated myself. "Breasts and no dick equals not male."

"The nectar has never failed us," Brunner replied calmly. "It identifies the gene and manifests the mark. You have the mark, which means, as unorthodox as it may seem, somehow you have the gene."

"Ines?" Melle said. "You really think a woman could have the gene? After all this time."

"I believe there's an explanation for everything." She smiled tightly at me. "I've sent a messenger to summon your parents. We'll start there, and then move on to council advice if need be. I'd rather not escalate the issue if, by some chance, there has been an error." She fixed her attention on Master Herman.

The Herbs and Toxins master shook his head. "No. No, the nectar was brewed to perfection."

Principle Brunner canted her head as if listening for something. "I believe your parents have arrived."

The door to the office opened a moment later, and my father strode in, dressed in all his Armani finery. His distinctive cologne filled the room and turned my stomach. I clenched my teeth.

A diminutive woman tottered in on six-inch heels

behind him. My mother. Perfectly coiffed and powdered. She was a beauty, and she knew it.

Master Herman didn't even bother to hide his gawp.

Her gaze fell on me, and there was a flash of something akin to concern, but it was so fleeting I was sure I'd imagined it.

"What has she done now?" my father asked Brunner.

His words had me curling my hands into fists.

"Baron, please take a seat," Brunner said with a smile. "Indigo hasn't done anything. It's more what has happened to her that concerns us."

My father didn't even look at me. "I'm sure whatever it was, she brought it on herself. My daughter has a penchant for attracting trouble. Anything for attention."

"Mr. Justice—"

"Whatever it is, I suggest you take it with a pinch of salt and send her back to her dorms."

"It's not that simple. I—"

"I know what this is." My father took a step closer to Brunner's desk. "You're trying to get rid of her. Use this incident, whatever it is, to force her out of the Academy. Well, let's get something straight. We have a deal in place. The council has put her in your care for the next three years. It's your job to keep her out of trouble. To train her and shape her."

"Like you failed to do?" Hyde said, his tone low and menacing.

My father straightened and looked down his nose at Master Hyde. "I'd remember your place if I were you, Archer. Tenures can be cut short."

"And maybe you should bloody listen to what the principal has to say," Garnet snapped. "Instead of making incorrect assumptions." There was sympathy in her gaze when she turned it on me. "Show him, Indigo."

I kept my gaze averted because if I looked at him, if I met his eyes, I'd lose my shit and either scream in his face or burst into tears. The pressure building in my head and throat meant it could go either way. I pulled my tunic down far enough to reveal the mark.

Someone gasped.

My mother.

My gaze flicked her way to see her eyes bright and her mouth quivering. Taking a breath to rein in my emotions, I lifted my head to finally look at my father, needing to see his reaction.

His lips were bloodless, and his eyes were dark with anger, almost as if he was furious with me. Nothing new there. But how could he be mad at me over this?

He took a shuddering breath and fixed his attention on Brunner. "That's what *he* would have been then," he said softly. "That mark was *his* destiny."

Who was he talking about? "Mother?"

She slumped into the nearest seat, her hand covering her mouth.

Brunner looked from my mother to my father. "Mr. Justice, if you know something that can explain this, then please, enlighten us."

He cleared his throat. "Indigo was a twin. Partway into the pregnancy, she absorbed her brother. They call it vanishing twin syndrome in humans. They'd never seen it happen in a supernatural pregnancy before and there was no literature on it. No explanation as to how it happened. They said it meant our son was never meant to be. But it seems now he had a destiny of his own." He looked at me now, locked gazes with me, and there was so much vitriol in his eyes that my insides shriveled up, and any tiny hope of ever earning his love died. "A destiny *you* stole."

I felt the eyes of the room on me, the shock and the sympathy. Anger and despair rose up to choke me. I stood, toppling my chair.

"*That's* why you didn't love me? Why you treated me like an obligation rather than a fucking daughter? Because of something I had no control whatsoever over?" My voice rose incredulously. I looked to my mother. "What is wrong with you? You're my mother. You carried me in your womb for thirteen months. How can you not feel anything?"

She kept her head down and the urge to shake her

rose up to choke me. I took an involuntary step toward her. The door swung open, giving me the second I needed to get myself under control. Shit. What the fuck had I been about to do?

A familiar figure strode in. Master Payne froze and took in the scene, and then his gaze fell on my mother, and his mouth turned down as if in displeasure.

"Hello, Carter," my father said. "I see everyone is invited to witness the spectacle that just happens to be my daughter." He waved a hand in my direction.

Master Payne's gaze flicked to my chest then back to my mother.

She was looking up at him now. Her expression was soft. "Hello, Carter."

He nodded curtly. "Lea."

"So, Justice has the gene," Master Hyde said. "What now?"

My father spun on his heel and headed toward the door. "Not my problem. The deal still stands, except now you own her." He grinned over his shoulder as if this was some kind of twisted victory. "Not many shadow knights being born recently, are there? I doubt the council would want to lose a shadow knight that could protect thousands of humans over the lost life of one." He looked at me. "It looks like you've been given a chance to redeem yourself. Don't mess it up." He clicked his fingers. "Come, Lea."

My mother looked torn, and for a moment I thought she'd come to me, hug me, something. But with a final lingering glance at Master Carter, she followed my father from the room.

Silence descended like a shroud.

I could feel them watching me—the girl who'd absorbed her sibling in the womb. Who'd killed her brother. No wonder my parents hated me. A wave of emotions smashed into me, and I took a staggered step back. It pooled in my chest and then hardened into a rock that pressed onto my heart. My eyes burned and stung.

No. Like hell would I cry.

I raised my chin and glared daggers at everyone in the room. "Stop it. Stop looking at me."

"Justice, I'm so sorry," Brunner said softly.

Garnet nodded, her mouth twisted in sympathy.

Fuck them and their pity. I swallowed the lump in my throat. "What now? What happens to me now?"

"Too many students saw the mark," Garnet said to Brunner.

"I know," Brunner replied.

Wait ... no. They couldn't seriously expect me to go through with this. "Then tell them it was a mistake. Get rid of the damn thing. You have weavers. Get them to hide it. I didn't come here for this."

But no one was listening to me.

"We can't turn our backs on this and pretend it's not happening," Garnet said. "She's an anomaly—a woman with the gene. We need to explore this."

Brunner pouted in thought. "If we let this go, then the conscription law will be questioned."

"Then we conscript her," Hyde said, his intense gaze on me. "She has the gene, so she has the power."

"Hyde," Payne said. "Maybe we need to stop and think about this."

"Thank you!" I threw my hands up.

"There's no other option," Brunner said. "It's what the council would want."

For God's sake. "Doesn't it matter what the fuck I want?"

"No." Hyde narrowed his gaze. "In the forest the other day when the youngling attacked, what was your first instinct?"

Huh? "Fight." Where was he going with this? "It's always to fight."

He nodded. "Then you belong with us. Pack your things, and make your way to the shadow cadet dorms."

Damn it.

"Um, Archer," Melle said. "The dorm is male only."

"There's an empty room on the tutor floor. She can have that," Archer said. "That way, I can keep an eye on her."

He meant, make sure none of the horny boys bugged me. They'd made up their mind. I was trapped, and there was no getting out of this.

I grit my teeth. "I can take care of myself."

"I'm sure you can," Hyde replied. "But the shadow cadets are my responsibility, and now that you wear the mark, so are you." His smile was brittle. "Forget what you've learned so far. Your real training starts tomorrow."

THIRTEEN

The corridors were empty on the way back to the nightblood and moonkissed wing. It looked like festivities had been cut short. Everyone probably knew about my mark now. News spread like chocolate spread on hot crumpets in this place. And news about the criminal was a gossip mill staple. I'd kept a low profile and refused to feed it the past few weeks, but now my name would be on everyone's lips as they speculated over why I had the mark.

I'd just gone from criminal to freak.

I turned the corner onto my floor and slammed into a wide chest. My palms came up to brace against taut muscle.

A hand shot out to steady me. "Indie?"

I looked up into Harmon's perpetual five o'clock shadow and the concerned face beneath. "That's me."

"What happened?" he asked.

I glanced down at the bulging bag in his hand.

He followed my gaze. "All shadow marked have been instructed to move into the shadow wing." There was a question in his cocoa eyes.

I swallowed the lump in my throat. "Yeah. Me too."

He blew out a breath. "So, it's real? The mark?"

"What's real?" Thomas appeared behind Harmon. "Indie, shit. The mark is legit?"

I nodded. "I don't want to talk about it. I've got to pack and ... move."

Thomas looked torn for a moment. "Do you want us to wait for you?"

Was Thomas being nice to me? I narrowed my eyes. "Did you just offer to do something for me that didn't involve mockery or humiliation?"

Harmon and Thomas exchanged an uncomfortable look.

I guess now wasn't the time to call them out on all the shitty stuff said to me over the last two months.

I threw up my hands. "It's fine. I'm fine."

"Of course you are."

I looked over my shoulder to see Oberon descending on me, wrath blazing in his eyes.

"You took it. You took my mark." He grabbed my shoulder, fingers digging into my flesh, and swung me round to face him. "Give it back."

He lunged for the neck of my top but didn't make it because Harmon's fist was kissing his face. Oberon stumbled back, clutching his nose.

"Back off, man." Thomas planted himself between Harmon and Oberon. "Trust me, you do not want to piss Harmon off."

Harmon was positively vibrating with rage, but my attention was fixed on Oberon. Cool, calm, collected Oberon who had in the space of a few hours turned into a raging, paranoid lunatic.

He met my gaze, and the crazy sheen in his eyes ebbed. His shoulders slumped. "It's over," he said. "I failed." He walked away without another word.

Thomas turned to me. "Way to take things personally."

"He's an idiot," Harmon said. "He actually wants this shit." He made a sound of disgust deep in his throat.

"Are you okay?" Thomas asked me, and yes, that was genuine concern on his slender face.

"Why are you being nice to me?"

He blinked sharply in surprise and then had the grace to look sheepish. "Because things are different now. We're in this together, and the rest of the world ... what they think ... It doesn't matter."

"It shouldn't have mattered in the first place. Funny how it takes a death mark for you to decide to start thinking for yourself." He ducked his head, and my anger melted. "Forget it. Look, I'll see you in a bit. I need to ... to say goodbye to Minnie." My throat tightened.

Harmon nodded. "Okay. I'm going to dump my

stuff in the new digs then come back to check on Lottie. She didn't make it to the ceremony. Probably getting into some shit somewhere." His gaze roved over my face, probing. "If you're still about when I get back, I'll walk back with you."

Harmon Black was offering an escort. I can't say I wasn't tempted. I wasn't worried about Oberon showing up and trying to get a look at the mark on my boob, him I could have handled if Harmon had given me a chance. It was more that stepping into the shadow wing alone didn't appeal. Also, Thomas and Harmon being nice to me was too much change too quickly. This empathy, this understanding. It was alien, and it made me want to scream.

I grit my teeth. "I'm good. Thanks."

Harmon's jaw tensed. "Fine. See you later."

They strode off, and guilt stabbed at me. Maybe I should have accepted Harmon's offer. It was too late now, though. Best to just get this exit over with.

Minnie leapt off her bed as I entered. "What the heck happened?"

Harper perched on the edge of the bed, curiosity painted across her neatly made-up face. Even though I knew she cared about Minnie, and yeah, I felt bad about possibly coming in between them, right now, I needed to be alone with my friend.

I kept my attention on Minnie as I spoke. "Harper, can you please give us a minute?"

Harper had the grace not to argue. "Come knock

for me later," she said to Minnie. There was a confidence in her tone that had been absent the last time we'd spoken.

She knew she'd won. She knew that I was being forced out of Minnie's orbit.

The door closed softly behind her.

"Indie?" Minnie nudged.

I stood hands on hips. "I don't even know where to start." It was too much, too quick. Too many revelations. "I have to pack. They're moving me to the shadow cadet wing."

"What?" She took a breath to steady herself. "No. Of course. You have the mark." Her eyes were filled with questions. "How? How can you have the mark?"

"Because I killed my brother in the womb." The words came out in a rush.

"You what?"

I pressed my lips together and grabbed my suitcase from under the bed. "I absorbed him." I flung open my wardrobe. "And that's why my parents hate me. I'm not a son, and I'm the killer of their son." I piled clothes into the case. "This mark belonged to him."

Minnie gasped. "His genes ... You have his genes."

"Yep."

"Do you feel ... different? I mean more shadow knighty?"

Shadow knighty? I stopped with my favorite jeggings clutched in my hand. *Did* I feel different?

Amidst all the commotion and disclosures, I'd

blocked out the changes in my body. But now that Minnie mentioned it, there was a new energy thrumming through my veins. No ... Not new. It was familiar—the surge I got when I was running, the golden adrenaline rush of a fight. This energy was an old friend, but one who'd been cloaked until now. Now it filled me. It completed me.

"Indie?"

"I feel ... stronger. Better." God that sounded weak. "I can't explain it."

"No. Neither could Lloyd." She smiled softly. Sadly. "You're one of them now."

She walked over to my wardrobe and grabbed a pile of clothes. "You have to fold them, or they'll crease."

Yeah, I was not a folder.

I hadn't brought a lot, and it took minutes to pack up, and then we stood facing each other and the enormity of what was happening hit me hard in the solar plexus. This, us, was over. I was being confined to the shadow camp, to a life of servitude to the shadow knights. No option to leave. No option to decline. I might have escaped execution, but I'd been thrust into a life sentence that, more often than not, ended prematurely in a painful death.

And Minnie, my friend, my lifeline here, was being taken from me.

She scanned my face as if reading my thoughts. "No. Na-uh. We're friends, and just because you have to live in the shadow wing and do shadow shit doesn't mean we can't still hang out."

"We won't have any of the same lessons."

"So, we meet up at lunch and after class."

"Do the shadow cadets even get to have downtime?"

Her expression said it all. My stomach felt queasy.

"We'll make time. We'll find a way." Her expression was earnest, and hope bloomed in the despair.

Maybe we could still see each other. Maybe things didn't have to be so ... serious. "Yeah. Yeah, fuck it. This is *not* the end."

She hugged me. "Maybe ... if you let it. It could be a beginning."

A shiver skated up my spine at her words.

She pulled back. "Come on. I'll walk you to the east wing."

THE TEMPERATURE DROPPED as we reached the shadow wing, and Minnie's grip on my hand tightened.

Before coming here, I'd never had a friend to hold my hand. The most physical contact I'd had was when I'd been beating on someone or grappling with them in a wrestling match.

Minnie had turned me soft.

The archway that led to the shadow wing was closed off by sturdy oak doors. I tried the handle and rattled it to no avail. Locked. An intercom sat snug in the stone wall beside it.

I pressed the buzzer and waited.

"Name?" The voice was male and sounded slightly bored.

"Indigo Justice."

"Ah. Yes. The anomaly. Do come on up."

The door clicked, and when I tried the handle again, it opened easily.

"So, I guess this is goodbye for now." Minnie pressed her lips together, and her eyes glittered with tears.

"I swear, Min. If you cry …"

"Fuck that!" She waved a dismissive hand. "See you at lunch tomorrow?"

We hugged, and then I slipped through the door and into the shadow wing.

A STONE STAIRCASE lit by electric wall sconces led up to the floor above. The walls were bare gray stone too, and a heavy chill pervaded the air, but thanks to my nightblood constitution, it didn't really affect me. In fact, my body was pleasantly warm.

An effect of the activation of the shadow knight gene, maybe?

Did it affect the feyblood shadow cadets the same?

It would have to for them to cope with these arctic temperatures.

I reached the top of the staircase and stepped into a huge foyer area. Three doors led off it. One was unmarked, the others had copper signs marked cadet quarters and master quarters.

Master Hyde had said I'd be staying in the tutor wing, so maybe ... I reached for the master quarters' door just as it swung open, and a figure stepped through. Four-foot tall, with pointy ears, slanted cat's eyes, and strange tiger stripe markings slanting down from his hair line across his forehead, the creature was unlike anything I'd ever seen. And that hair ... Impressively gelled and funky. The strange-looking man-creature looked up at me and then let out a purr.

I backed up.

He stepped into the hallway and canted his head to study me curiously. He was dressed in dark purple velvet trousers and a black shirt, and his hands were paw-like and hairy. Shit, was that a tail curling over his shoulder?

I locked gazes with his eerie slit-pupiled one. "What are you?"

He advanced, and I held my ground.

"Well, that's a fine way to address your dorm master, isn't it?" he drawled, circling me. His tail flicked about distractingly. "Yes, yes, you certainly have the scent of a shadow knight."

Feyblood maybe? I'd never seen anything like him.

He canted his head. "And you won't."

"Wait? What? Did you just—"

"Read your mind? Yes. Yes, I did. An unfortunate side effect of you thinking too loudly. Tone it down."

I had to think of something else, anything else but how much like a cat he looked. A cute kitty cat with … with a human face. Oh, God. This was too weird.

He blinked slowly at me. "I do not look like a cat. Cats look like me."

"Okay, stop that."

"You're the one broadcasting your thoughts. You need to calm down. Rein in your confusion."

I took a deep breath and exhaled.

"Good … very good. I can't hear your thoughts at all now." He smirked.

"You're lying, aren't you?"

"Undoubtedly."

"Larkin?" Master Hyde stepped through the door. "Has Justice—" He caught sight of me hovering by the staircase. "Good, you're here, and you've met Larkin, the dorm master. He runs the shadow wing, so if you need anything you can—"

"Find me in the turret room in the masters' wing." He did one final circle around me, and this time, his tail brushed the back of my neck, and then he was headed for the stairs.

"Too yummy, Archer, much too yummy." He purred.

Master Hyde's jaw tensed. "And a cadet."

Larkin glanced over his shoulder. "I am the epitome of morality." He dropped me a wink and then leapt forward onto all fours and bounded up the stairs.

I stared after him.

"Close your mouth, Justice," Hyde snapped. "Ignore what I said earlier. If you need anything, you come to me." He turned his broad back on me. "This way."

Another damn staircase and another floor.

"What is he?"

"Larkin? An Otherworlder. He's old. Not sure how old he is. He's been part of the Watch forever."

"He looks ... feline."

"And he hates it. So, don't bring it up."

"Too late."

"Hurumph." He pushed open a door at the end of a hallway. "Our quarters are through here."

There was a narrow corridor and two doors facing each other.

He indicated the door to the left. "This is your room. Key's inside. Linens in the closet. Make yourself comfortable. There's a sink in your room, but the bathroom's down the hall. It locks. Training begins at nine p.m. sharp, and we meet in the lobby at eight-thirty p.m. sharp."

"I can do sharp."

He arched a brow and raked me with his strange blue-green cocktail eyes flecked with gold. Cyan was the closest color to what his eyes were, but even that didn't describe the shade adequately.

"I'm sure you can," he said. "But being a shadow knight isn't like jumping into a pit fight, Justice. Being a knight takes discipline, graft, and heart."

He knew about my pit fights? Well, then he needed to know the rest. "You think pit fighting doesn't require discipline and heart?" I glared up at him. "I'm a trained boxer. I can wrestle, I can fence, and I'm perfectly at home using a variety of swords and daggers. I may not have trained in some prestigious establishment and picked up medals and certificates, but I can hold my own in a fight. I don't go down easy. When I finally get into that mist, those fomorians better watch out."

His eyes darkened a fraction, and then the corner of his mouth curved up in half a smile, and I was suddenly, acutely, and painfully aware that we were standing almost chest to chest in a gloomy enclosed space. There wasn't enough oxygen in the air or enough saliva in my mouth.

And I was staring, just fixated on his lips. Shit. I tore my gaze up and got caught in the hunger in his eyes. He blinked, and it was gone.

He stepped back. "Get some rest, cadet. You'll be taking your oath tomorrow, and then we'll be headed to sector one for orientation."

"Sector one?"

But he was already disappearing down the

corridor, leaving me internally gasping outside my new dorm room.

"You're thinking too loud ..."

The voice drifted down the corridor. I reached behind me, twisted the handle, and tumbled into my room, slamming the door shut behind me.

It was time to get off the emotional rollercoaster.

MY NEW ROOM was smaller than the dorm room I'd shared with Minnie. Bare wooden floors. A single bed in need of sheets and a barred window. Nice. A dresser, small wardrobe, sink, and mirror completed the room.

I got the impression this room would simply be a place to crash after training. From what I'd heard, the shadow cadets didn't get much downtime.

I dropped my bag on the floor and headed to the wardrobe to grab the sheets. Half an hour later, the bed was made, and my clothes were put away. The clock winked at me, showing it to be two a.m. Three hours till dawn. Time to put on my sleep shorts and ratty T-shirt.

Minnie and I would have been snuggled in bed by now, whispering about our day before falling into slumber. God, I missed her.

A sharp rap sounded on the door.

"Justice."

Master Hyde? I opened the door to find him

dressed in dark combat gear. "Is something the matter?"

His gaze fell to my bare legs, and he took a step away from the doorway. "We have a missing student." He handed me a bundle of dark clothing. "Get dressed, and be in the foyer in five. We're organizing a search party."

He made to turn away.

"Who is it? Who's missing."

He glanced over his shoulder. "A student named Lottie Black."

FOURTEEN

The clothes were too big, obviously made for a guy. I tucked and tightened best I could, shoved on my boots, scraped back my hair, and made it into the foyer in less than four minutes.

The space was already filled with bodies and the urgent buzz of conversation. I caught sight of Harmon's tousled dark head and shoved through the crowd to get to him. Shocked glances were thrown my way.

"What's a woman doing here?" someone said.

I guess not all the cadets knew about my arrival.

"Hey." Someone grabbed my elbow.

I turned on the guy with a scowl to find Lloyd looking down on me with a concerned frown. "Indigo, what are you doing here?"

I grabbed the collar of my ribbed top and pulled it down to reveal my mark. "Got conscripted earlier."

Shock sparked in his icy blue eyes, and then he released me abruptly. "Back up. She's one of us."

"What?"

"The fuck?"

Disconcertion rippled across the room. But the crowd parted to let me through, and Harmon's cocoa gaze fell on me as I approached. "I couldn't find her earlier," he said. "I should have known something was wrong. I just thought she was fucking about as usual. I should have reported it earlier."

"She's probably ducked out with some friends," Thomas said. "Smoking poppy seed cigarettes, off site."

"Everyone else is accounted for," Harmon said through gritted teeth. He shot Thomas an irritated look. "We wouldn't be organizing a fucking search party otherwise."

"Maybe Redmond lost another youngling, and the cadet ended up being its supper," someone to our left said.

Harmon growled and lunged at the second year, who blocked him easily before shoving him back. "Watch it!"

I stepped between them. "It's his sister, okay. The missing girl is his sister."

The second year glanced at me, then back at Harmon, and then his body relaxed. "I'm sorry, man. I've got a big mouth. We'll find her, okay."

Harmon's chest heaved, but he stood down and nodded.

"Listen up!" Master Hyde's voice cut through the hubbub. "We take the tunnels, and we split up into three groups. There's a shirt being passed around that belongs to the girl. Moonkissed, take a whiff. Faraday, Toller, take the newbies. Spinner and Goyle, split the rest. Faraday, comb the southeast and southwest grounds. Goyle, the outer forest, and Spinner, northeast and northwest grounds. Got it?"

"Yes, Master Hyde," the cadets said in unison.

"Newbies, get your arses over here." Lloyd held up a hand, and the crowd began to shift.

Harmon, Thomas, and I followed the new cadets to stand around Lloyd.

"The tunnels are a maze if you're not used to them, so stay close," he warned.

"What tunnels?" one of the new cadets asked.

"You'll see soon enough."

The foyer was emptying out as the second-year cadets made their way through the unmarked door and out of sight.

"Follow me." Lloyd headed toward the door, and Harmon was the first to follow. "The tunnels span several miles beneath the academy grounds. We use them to get to the training grounds, into the forest and up to the fortress, and into the mist."

"Wait, what?" Thomas asked.

"They haven't taken their oath yet," Toller reminded Faraday.

"They're conscripted, Toller," Faraday said. "The oath is just a formality now."

The two second years led us through the door and down a flight of stone steps. Dank and moist air drifted up to meet us, and old-style scones lit up as we passed. Weaver magic?

We hit the ground and hurried down a tunnel wide enough to walk two by two. Harmon fell into step beside me with Thomas behind. The tension was palpable as it pressed in on us.

Could Lottie have been attacked by a youngling? Redmond had been so sure he had that situation under control. But what if he'd been wrong?

We took several turns, and I noted the markings on the wall—arrows and symbols. Directions?

We passed an arch that led to another tunnel, even more dimly lit than the one we were already in, and then cool, fresh air caressed my cheek, and we were piling out of a wooden door, up an earthy incline, pushing through shrubbery, and out into the starlit sky.

The exit had brought us up on the other side of the training grounds. The tunnel behind us was neatly hidden by the bushes we'd just stepped through.

Clever.

"Fan out and search the area," Lloyd said. "Only two hours till dawn. Let's find the Nightwatch cadet."

To the left was the outdoor herb garden, and to the

right, the glass roof of the hothouse was visible. Several cadets ran off toward the gardens.

"Let's check out the hothouse." I jogged off in the opposite direction.

Harmon was on high alert, sniffing the air. "I can't smell anything. The air is off."

"What do you mean?" Thomas said.

Nightbloods had excellent senses, but we couldn't beat the moonkissed sense of smell.

"It should smell of earth and pollen and life, but there's a musky scent in the air that's masking it all."

I inhaled deeply. "Yeah ... I smell it. Weird."

We slowed, taking in the surroundings. No point looking for prints, too much foot traffic there. The ground was part grass and part mud. Scent was our best bet at finding Lottie, but with the strange masking effect on the air, it wasn't going to be easy.

We were outside the hothouse when a cry went up.

"I found something! A shoe. I found a shoe."

"Blood!" someone else shouted.

Harmon turned and ran toward the voices.

Thomas made to follow, but I grabbed his arm.

I shook my head. "Wait. They found a shoe and blood. They haven't found her. We should check out the hothouse, just in case."

Thomas looked torn but then nodded and followed me into the hothouse. Warm, humid air blasted in our faces. The hothouse was a huge structure filled with delicate and exotic blooms and herbs. Flower beds to the left and long tables holding herb pots to the right. This was Master Herman's domain. Maybe he was here somewhere?

The place was large enough to get lost in, but we'd barely gone a few meters in when I caught sight of a shoeless foot sticking out from behind a table.

My heart skipped a beat, and I rushed toward the figure. "Lottie." I crouched by her unconscious form and did a quick sweep of her. No visible injury. "Lottie." I shook her shoulder gently.

"I'll get Harmon." Thomas turned and ran for the exit.

Lottie looked calm and serene like she was simply sleeping. They'd found a shoe and blood. Was the blood hers? Moonkissed healed fast too, so the wound could simply have knitted.

Shit.

"Lottie." I lifted her head into my lap. "Wake up."

Her eyelids fluttered, and she moaned softly. "Whaa ..."

"Lottie, hey. You're okay."

She opened her eyes and stared up at me.

I smiled reassuringly. "Hey, what happened. How did you get here?"

She blinked slowly, her gaze sharpening.

"Lottie!" Harmon came barreling in and fell to his knees beside us. He gathered his sister into his arms and squeezed. "Shit. You scared the life out of me." He pulled back to look into her face. "What happened? How did you get here?"

Lottie stared up at his face. "Where am I?"

"The hothouse," Harmon said.

"You were unconscious," Thomas added.

Master Hyde appeared behind Harmon.

"We should get her back to the med bay."

Harmon made to scoop her up, but she cringed and backed up into me. "No. Don't touch me. Who are you?" She stared in confusion at Harmon, then up at Thomas and the other shadow cadets hovering behind him. "Who are you people?"

Harmon paused in his action. "Lottie, it's me. Harmon. Your brother."

Her expression was pained. "Lottie? Who? ... I don't know you."

"Back away from her," Master Hyde said.

"Like hell," Harmon growled. "She's my sister. She probably banged her head. She's confused." He made to scoop her up again.

Lottie opened her mouth and screamed.

FIFTEEN

My eyes snapped open to a blood-red room as the sun went down. I swung my legs out of bed, grabbed my shower stuff, and headed out the door. I needed to get dressed and find Harmon and Thomas before training.

I needed to know how Lottie was doing.

Master Hyde had rushed Lottie to the med bay while Harmon stood stock-still, his face a mask of torment.

She didn't remember him. Didn't remember us. Didn't fucking remember anything.

They were holding her in the med bay while they tried to figure out what had happened to her.

But one thing was clear, people didn't just lose their memories and their identities. Something had done this to her, and it was still out there. I needed to check on Harmon and find out what the hell they were doing about Lottie.

He was an ass most of the time, but he was hurting right now, and for some reason, I wanted to be there for him.

Shower bag and clothes in hand, I headed out of my room and down the short corridor to the bathroom. The door opened before I could turn the handle, and Master Hyde stepped out wreathed in steam. His torso was bare and beaded with moisture. Droplets skated down his powerful chest, over the ink that wound its way across his pectoral to skim the base of his neck. Droplets skidded over his eight-pack and down to kiss the lip of the towel hugging the V at his hips.

Heat climbed up from my toes and blossomed in my head. I tore my gaze up to his face, and my breath locked in my throat. Beads of water hovered on his lips and lashes, they licked at his scars, softening them somewhat. But it was his hooded gaze that trapped me. There was heat hidden in the depths, a dangerous devastation that called to me, inviting me to drown in it.

"It's all yours." His voice was gruff, as if these were his first words of the evening.

His tone had a delicious abrasiveness that rubbed against my senses and made my skin tingle with the need to be touched.

He made to step around me and his citrus scent hit

me, short-circuiting my brain. I sidestepped to block him. Fuck. Wrong way. We both stepped the other way, once again blocking each other.

Shit.

"Stop." His hands came up and cupped my shoulders.

The heat of his hands seeped through my shirt and kissed my skin, making it blush. My breath caught and then I was trapped in his blue-green gaze, being pulled into the darkness of his darkening pupils.

"Don't move." His voice was low and husky.

My body leaned toward him as he passed, but then the heat of his hands was gone. He stepped around me, leaving me staring at air.

I looked over my shoulder to see raised welts edged in puckered scar tissue. They crisscrossed his back, telling a horrific story.

Were these wounds from the attack that had taken his leg? And if so, why hadn't they completely healed? My attention dropped to his legs, and there it was—the glint of metal, gold and silver entwined into the shape of a powerful limb. It didn't look mechanical, but then it was feytech, so ...

He stopped and turned his head, offering me his profile. "Had a good look?"

"I'm ... I'm sorry." My voice cracked.

"Don't be. Survival is nothing to be sorry about." I caught the corner of his mouth lift slightly. "And a feytech leg is better than two flesh and bone ones." He strode off, taking his bionic limb and his compelling scars with him.

But he took my breath with him too and left me standing there with my heart in my mouth and my body blazing with the heat of desire.

The bathroom door shut firmly behind me, and I leaned up against it. His citrus scent was infused in the steamy air. His scars were burned into my mind. He was damaged, but he was far from broken, and that, to me, was beautiful.

Fuck. I'd need to take my shower cold.

THE SHADOW CADET quarters were an open lounge space with several corridors shooting off from it. The lounge also had a small kitchenette area with a counter that ran around it to separate it from the seating area. My feet dragged me across the wood floor, lured by the smell of coffee that permeated the air.

A golden-haired figure stood with his back to me at the coffee pot.

I'd recognize those broad shoulders and slender hips anywhere.

Lloyd looked over his shoulder, sensing my approach. "Early bird?"

I crossed my arms, not sure how to gauge his tone. It sounded neutral enough, but Lloyd had never been anything but dismissive and derisive of me, so waiting for the other shoe to drop was standard procedure when it came to him.

I hung back, keeping the counter between us. "I was hoping to check on Harmon."

Lloyd spooned sugar into his mug. "He and Thomas left a few minutes ago. I assume they're heading to the med bay before training." He turned back to his coffee-making task.

I cleared my throat. "How did he look?"

"Tense, worried." He turned to me and leaned up against the counter behind him. "All the things a brother might look like if his sister had just lost her memories." He ran a hand over his face. "I'm not sure I'd be as calm as he is."

He turned away to pour milk into his coffee and then carried his mug into the lounge area.

I took his place at the coffee pot and poured hot, fragrant wonderfulness into a mug. "This smells amazing."

"Yeah. Larkin gets it imported from somewhere or other. Specially for the shadow cadets."

I took a sip and couldn't help the involuntary moan of pleasure that escaped my lips. "God, that's good."

Lloyd's attention was on my mouth, but he looked away quickly when my gaze flicked to his face.

He and Minnie had the same almond-shaped eyes, but whereas hers were a warm jade, his were a cool blue. There were very few similarities between them, aside from that. Lloyd had sharp, harsh features that some would find compelling, but I'd always found haughty. But the way he was studying me now was devoid of his usual contempt. In fact, there was a spark of interest there that had my insides squirming with confusion.

"What?" I held my coffee mug like a shield. "Why are you looking at me like that?"

He shook his head and took a gulp of his coffee. "Nothing. You better get to the dining hall." He jerked his head toward the corridor to my far left.

"You have your own dining hall?" That would explain why I rarely saw shadow cadets in the Nightwatch Academy dining room.

"Grab a bite. You have your oath, then sector one orientation today. You'll probably be late for lunch."

Master Hyde had mentioned sector one last night. "What is that? What is sector one?"

A slow smile curved his lips. "Oh, you'll see."

"Got the coffee on, Faraday?" A dark-haired guy with tousled waves falling into his eyes ambled into the lounge followed by three others.

The one directly behind him could have been his twin. Hang on ... he was his twin. They had the same twinkling hazel eyes and pouty mouths, but the one behind was stockier, as if he worked out more. The guy directly behind stocky dude was slight and wiry with sandy hair that was cut short at the back and sides but left longer on top. He yawned, showcasing even, white teeth with a hint of fang. The final guy kept his head down, but it was impossible to miss the claw marks on the side of his neck. Red angry welts cut down and vanished into the collar of his T-shirt. He caught me staring and bared his teeth in a growl.

"Back off, Brady," Lloyd said evenly.

Brady's lip curled, and he slumped into the nearest seat, his angry eyes fixed on my face as if daring me to stare, to speak, to breathe.

I glared back at him. Like hell would I let him intimidate me. He was big, but I'd taken down bigger.

His dark eyes narrowed, assessing me, and then he reached up to scratch at his stubble, and the stare-off was broken.

By him.

Ha.

"Ignore Brady," the slender twin said. "He's a beast until he's had his morning brew." The other twin passed him a steaming mug.

Brady took a long swig and sighed. His shoulders relaxed, and the rage in his expression ebbed a little.

"I'm Aidan," the slender twin said. "And this is my brother, Devon."

Devon grunted at me and ran a hand through his thick, dark hair.

"Carlo." The fair-haired guy smiled. "Is it true you ate your brother in the womb?"

The coffee I'd just sipped went down the wrong hole, and I ended up coughing it back up. My eyes watered, and I blinked back the sting of embarrassed anger.

"Fucking hell, Carlo," Brady grumbled. "They should fucking teach you some tact."

"Says the dude who growls to greet people," Carlo sing-songed.

I took a deep breath and stood tall. "I got the gene from my twin, yes." I stared them down one by one. "Anything else you want to know?"

"Shame you didn't also get his penis," Carlo said.

"You think a woman can't do the job?"

He shook his head. "Nah, you have the gene, you can do the job. But this is a male-dominated environment. Throw in a beautiful woman, and things are gonna get crazy."

Beautiful. Me? I filed that away for later examination. Possibly in front of a mirror. "I can take care of myself."

He chuckled. "I'm sure you can, but the cadets who'll be forced to bunk with you will be wondering how they can get you to take care of them."

What the ... My neck heated.

He held up his hands. "It's a lonely road. No women till we retire after twenty years of service. It's a *hard* life, if you catch my drift." He winked.

They didn't get to have sex?

Lloyd tutted. "It's not that bad. Shadow knights get the odd day's leave when we can portal to the mortal world and ... indulge." He cleared his throat. "But relationships and marriage have to wait till retirement. If we make it that far."

The guys flopped down onto the sofa against the wall, nursing mugs of brew.

"Are you sure you want to do this?" Aidan asked me.

"Not like she gets a fucking choice," Brady said.

I took a measured sip of my coffee this time. "I can handle myself and whatever comes at me."

"Comes ..." Carlo sniggered.

"Seriously, dude, grow the fuck up," Brady snarled. "Fucking twenty-year-old virgin."

Carlo sobered immediately. "Hey. What? No." He held up his hands and looked to me. "I am not a virgin."

The guys chuckled, and the tension that had pervaded the air eased. Long moments of companionable silence passed. This wasn't so bad. I mean, if these guys could be okay with a woman in the ranks then—

"What did you do?" Carlo's attention was on the cuffs at my wrist. The shackles that prevented me from escaping this place.

I looked down at them. Heck. I'd almost forgotten they were there. "I killed a human."

Saying the words out loud, simple and devoid of excuses, felt good.

Carlo held my gaze and nodded. "Sucks, doesn't it?"

"You say that as if you can relate."

Carlo lifted his hand and pulled back the arm of his gown. A silver cuff circled his wrist. "What? You thought you were the only criminal ever to get relegated to the Academy?" He grinned. "Legacy family move, baby. We fuck up, they shove us here."

"Legacy?"

"Harwood." He winked. "If you'd hung out in the social circles, there is no way you'd have missed my moves."

Aidan groaned and shook his head. "Here we go with the moves. You have two left feet on the dance floor; you know it, we all know it."

But my mind was on his previous statement. My father had known transferring a sentence to the Academy could be done. He'd manipulated events to get me here, to trap me here, and he'd been confident his plan would work because it had worked for others before him.

I wanted to ask Carlo how it had happened for him? If he remembered, if he had been conscious, in control, something. But the words stuck in my throat as the memory of what I'd done filled my mind.

"Don't," Carlo said. "Waste of fucking time. You can't change it. You can't change what you are. Just got to live with it." He peered at me from under lashes the color of wet sand. "I heard you used to kick ass in the pits. True?"

Oh, good. Solid ground. "Yeah. I fought in the pits."

"In that case," Devon said, his voice surprisingly soft for his size, "welcome to the gang. You need to be a fighter to survive here."

"These guys are my troop," Lloyd said. "We're in sector two training at the moment."

An ominous silence fell over the group, and my gaze traveled back to the claw marks on Brady's neck.

I had to know. "Is that where you got those?"

He didn't even bother to look up at me. "Got lucky."

The twins were moonkissed, Carlo was nightblood, and Brady was ... feyblood. We all healed fast, but Master Hyde had scars, and the wound on Brady looked fresh.

I set my mug on the counter. "The wounds never heal completely, do they?"

Brady did look up at me now. His jaw ticked, but it was Lloyd that answered.

He lifted his shirt to showcase claw marks across his abdomen—neat, pale scar tissue.

"Scars are better than being dead," he said. He dropped the edge of his shirt. "Go get fed. You're going to need it."

"Sector one?" Carlo asked, brows raised.

"Yeah," Lloyd said. "Orientation for the newbies."

Aidan threw back his coffee. "Yeah, you're going to need a full stomach for that."

They stood as one as if they'd practiced it, and padded toward the corridor to the second-year dorms.

It was only as they were vanishing around the corner that their footwear registered.

They were all wearing gray, fluffy slippers.

The shadow gene binds us.
The shadow gene unites us.
We speak not of the mist and its secrets to anyone but our shadow brothers.
We speak not of our trials and tribulations to anyone but our shadow brothers.
The mist is sacred. Our task is sacred and unspoken.

THE OATH SPILLED from my lips with ease, and my voice mingled with the male timbres around me. Harmon's deep baritone united with Thomas's tenor as we repeated the words Master Hyde led with. The second years had already left for training, and only the new cadets remained.

Ten of us.

Only ten.

Brunner's statement about fewer shadow cadets being born came to mind. Ten out of a whole year of Nightwatch cadets seemed awfully low, especially when the class was sixty-five percent male.

A tingle passed over my skin with each line spoken. This was binding weaver power at work. I imagined if I tried to speak of shadow cadet stuff to

Minnie later, then the words probably wouldn't come.

We were stepping into another prison, even as we stood in the student lounge in two neat rows dressed in our cadet black and blue.

We repeated the words until Master Hyde nodded curtly.

"Done."

He paced back and forth in front of us. "You're here, but that doesn't mean that you'll still be here at the end of the year. Cadet training is faster and more intense. Nightwatch has three terms to a year. We have two, and in between, we work at the fortress. This is on-the-job training, and yes, survival rates are low. If you make it to graduation in two years, then you deserve to be here. Until then, consider this your probation. Shadow cadets may live at the Academy, but we operate on fortress rules. Up with the owl, and down with the lark. Got it?" He threw a glance our way but didn't wait for a response before continuing. This had all the makings of a rote speech. How many times had he given it? "Your first test is in less than three weeks. The shadow trials come in three stages, and each stage takes place in a different sector. Today, you'll be introduced to the terrain on which you'll be tested in three weeks' time."

"What's the test?" one of the cadets asked.

Master Hyde fixed his eyes on the speaker and canted his head. "Did I ask you to speak, cadet?" That tone froze the hairs on the nape of my neck.

The cadet who'd spoken blinked in surprise and swallowed hard. "I was just—"

The guy beside him elbowed him in the ribs.

A figure materialized behind Hyde. It was Larkin, and he was perched on the countertop, tail swishing slowly.

I wasn't the only cadet to balk at his appearance. Someone even cursed loudly. The cat-man had literally materialized out of thin air. He'd been invisible. He could read minds *and* be invisible. Shit. I'd be giving my room a serious sweep every night before bed from now on.

"Oh, come now, Hyde," Larkin drawled. "The boy doesn't know the rules yet." He hopped off the counter and approached the lineup. "Here's how it is, lads ..." His gaze snagged on me. "And ladies. You listen, you learn, and you train. You do the things that Master Hyde asks of you, and you may survive the next year. What you don't do is interrupt. What you don't do is ask questions before Master Hyde opens the floor to questions. Got it?"

No one said anything.

Larkin rolled his cat eyes. "That was a question in need of a response."

A soft chorus of *yes sirs* filled the room.

Master Hyde's lips curved in a cold, cutting smile. "Thank you for the informative interruption, Larkin." He turned his attention back to the group as a whole. "We'll be taking the tunnels to sector one today. Stay close. If you stray and get lost, then you're on your own. Any questions?"

I raised my hand.

"Justice?"

"Where is sector one?"

He locked gazes with me, his eyes more green than blue today, lit up with something akin to glee. "Sector one, like all the other sectors, is in the mist."

SIXTEEN

The mist. We were headed to the bloody mist.

We jogged through the tunnels after Master Hyde. He took a left instead of the right we'd taken yesterday, and then the tunnel went from gray stone to black. The murmur of whispered conversation echoed off the walls.

Harmon and Thomas were a little ahead of me. I picked up the pace, so I was right behind the pair.

"Hey, how's Lottie?"

Harmon didn't answer. Instead, he shot off, leaving me and Thomas behind.

Thomas didn't try and follow him, and instead, he fell into step beside me. "They wouldn't let him see her. Said she was too fragile for any visitors. They said it would upset her. She doesn't remember anything. Not this place, not her family, not her name. Harmon is fucked. He cried. I've never seen him cry before."

I couldn't imagine Harmon crying either. The guy was cocky and hard as nails. "Fuck. What the hell could do that to a person?"

"I don't know. I mean, the brain is crazy complicated. They have Madam Mariana on the case. She's gonna do her weaver thing, and see if she can extract any memories to piece together what happened to Lottie."

Maybe then we would have some answers. "It won't help Harmon to push people away."

Thomas snorted. "Seriously? This coming from you? Miss I-have-a-wall-around-me-that-has-a-Minnie-sized-hole-in-it."

"Point taken. But I'm messed up as shit. Harmon is … He has it together."

"You'd think so. But he's not the playboy everyone thinks he is. And when it comes to Lottie, he's a total softie. He sees her as his responsibility. His mum died five years ago, and he took over caring for his sister. The Black pack doesn't have time for females. Its focus is on the males. Women are baby-making machines. He insisted Lottie attend the Academy as soon as she hit seventeen so he could watch over her so that she could have a purpose other than bearing children for the pack. He wanted more for her."

And now she didn't even remember him.

Shit.

Cool air brushed my skin.

"I think we're almost there," Thomas said.

"The mist?"

"Fucking hell, right?"

The tunnel grew brighter, and then we were slowing down and coming to a halt. Hyde stood at a thick metal grated barrier. There was a winch system set up on the wall to one side. He grabbed the handle and began to turn it slowly. The grating began to lift.

"Exit is by winch," Hyde said. "But your entry is by biosignature." He ushered us under the partially raised grating.

I stepped out into the night air, onto soft grass that rose in a hillock. Sparse woodland lay on either side of us, cocooning the entrance to the tunnels. Stars winked down at us, and a waning moon hung heavy and bright in the sky.

A citrus scent tickled my nostrils, and then Hyde brushed past me. The contact was brief and through clothing, but my skin tingled regardless.

"This way," he ordered.

We followed him over the knoll, and the world beyond came into view. Flat land was home to a low, squat building with a stream running behind it, and beyond ... Beyond was a swirling mass of silver and gray.

"The mist ..." Thomas took an awed step forward.

We'd heard about it. We'd read about it. But seeing it this close ... Wow.

"We'll be headed into it soon enough," Hyde said. "You can stare at it then, from the inside. Come on." He jogged down the knoll and toward the squat gray building.

Neat rectangular windows stared back at us. The building was a box made of brick and metal that looked impregnable. A garage door trundled up as we approached, and a stocky bald man wearing overalls, boots, and a tool belt ambled out to greet us. He raised a gloved hand to Hyde and then looked us over.

"This it?" He didn't sound impressed.

"I'm afraid so," Hyde said.

"Slim pickings. Half of 'em will be dead in two years."

"I know."

They were speaking about us as if we weren't there. As if we were nothing but cannon fodder, and anger flared in my chest.

"Hey!" I stepped forward. "How about a little confidence? How about a little mentorship? That is what you're supposed to be offering, right?" My ire was all for Hyde. For the man who was supposed to make us into knights but was acting as if we didn't matter.

Hyde's jaw ticked. "Get the fuck back in line, Justice."

I was a cadet, and he was my tutor, but right then, I was just a woman who'd been pushed around too much. "For what? For a chance to die? Is that all this is? A little faith would be a great motivator, you know. How about you give us the fucking benefit of the doubt instead of treating us like we're already bloody dead?"

Hyde looked down his nose at me, and then he smiled, a cruel thin smile that filled my veins with frost.

"You want motivation? How about this. You speak out of turn again, and I will personally feed you to Redmond's hounds. Do you understand me?"

He wouldn't do that ... Would he? His gaze bore into me, demanding a response. And yeah, in that moment, I had no doubt he'd follow up on his word.

"Yes."

"Yes, what?" he snapped.

"Yes, sir."

His lip curled. "Get back in line."

Part of me wanted to push, to rebel. But the primal part, the part that recognized danger, complied by taking a step back.

Hyde's shoulders didn't relax, though. He jerked his head toward the building. "File into the barracks. Vince will be running orientation." His smile was wry. "Let's have a little excitement, people. You're about to learn the truth about the mist."

HE'D CALLED this place the barracks—a place to house soldiers. A place for us? Two long tables with bench seats filled one room. There was a kitchen and a dorm-like room with bunk beds and a communal shower room off to one side.

Cadets obviously stayed here.

My pulse quickened. Would *we* be expected to stay here? Lloyd and his troop said they worked sector two ... was that deeper in the mist? Were there other barracks like this one?

Vince led us into a room with plastic chairs and a whiteboard. "Sit."

Chairs scraped on lino, and when we were all seated, he crossed his arms and stared at us.

"You got the shit end of the stick. No doubt about it," he said, his voice like gravel. "It ain't no joke that not all of you will survive the next two years. Just how it is, I'm afraid. Me. I served my time. Fifteen years, I did."

He pulled up the sleeve to his gloved hand and showcased a metal arm. "Lost my arm five years ago. So, here I am, relegated to sector one barracks master. But you ain't here to listen to my story. You want to know what's out there." He grabbed a chair, dragged it to the front of the room, and sat. "I'm here to tell you. You see that mist?" He jerked his head toward the window. "It ain't natural. But it ain't fomorian either. It's man-made." He paused there to let that sink in.

There was a ripple of confusion which manifested into whispers.

"Yes, that's right. The magic mist is not magic. We make it. It's Winterlock Technology. They provide the Atmospheric Modifiers that are planted all over the place—twenty-five hundred acres of land between us and them. The AM posts churn out the shit that keeps the fomorians at bay, *but*"—he raised an index finger —"over the centuries some creatures have evolved to live in the mist. They call it their home, and those are the threats we work to keep off our land."

Wait, what? The fomorians couldn't get to us? We were safe?

"Hounds have adapted to the mist," Vince continued. "They roam in packs—huge fuckers with massive tear-you-the-fuck-to-shreds teeth. There are fucked-up mutant bugs and snakes. You got your biters too—humanoid critters that used to live on the other side but have built hives in the mist." He sat back with his hands relaxed in his lap. "The farther you go, the worse it gets. And then you have the raids. The fomorian bastards have found a way to withstand the mist for short periods of time. They send parties coated in some kinda fomorian clay to try and knock out the AM posts. They want to end the mist so they can swarm us. It's our job to keep the mist alive and to keep the number of threats in the mist to a minimum. We cull, we fix, we plant, and while out there, we're under constant threat." He took a deep breath and scanned our faces. His gaze locked on me for a long beat before moving on to Harmon. "Yeah, it's dangerous. Yeah, you might die. But fuck, you could get hit by a night bus crossing the street in the human realm and have had your life amount to squat. Here you get a chance to matter. Here death means something."

"If anyone can do this, you can. You were born stronger and faster with this purpose in mind. Regular supernaturals and humans would die beyond the mist. But your fomorian heritage allows you to thrive on both sides of the mist."

One of the cadets raised his hand.

"What?" Vince asked impatiently.

"If the mist can hurt fomorians, surely it should hurt us too?" the cadet pointed out.

Good point.

Vince grinned. "That's where that fucker Winterlock did his genius shit. The particles in the mist target and bond to aspects of fomorian DNA not found in shadow knights. They attack the fomorians on a genetic level. Incapacitate and kill them." He looked out the window again. "This sector will be your home for your first year. You'll take shifts in the barracks. You'll patrol it, and you'll make maintenance checks on the AM posts. Sector one is low threat, but it's also the last line of defense, so if any shit does get this far, you need to be prepared to bring it the fuck down. Got me?"

There was a low murmur of assent. I nodded, my mouth working with the others.

"So, let's kick off by getting you kitted out for the mist. The shit in the air disintegrates regular manmade fabric, so when out there, we wear Winterlock forged armor."

He stood and stretched his stocky form. "Come on then. Let's get ya fitted." He clomped off to the other end of the room and through a door.

There were dazed expressions, contemplative ones, and plain shocked ones—he'd just thrown a bunch of intel at us and not even allowed us to blink an eye before moving swiftly on. For a long beat, no one moved.

Fuck it. I pushed back my chair and stood. "I, for one, am ready to see what all the fuss is about." I strode after Vince, and the scrape of chairs being pushed back followed me.

HYDE WAS WAITING in the armor room. It had to be the armor room because there was a shed load of silver metallic breast plates and shoulder pieces hanging on hooks. A poster of a man wearing armor was pasted to the wall with neat labels identifying the different parts. There was a large wooden chest pushed up against the wall to the far left, and another wall was taken up by what looked like a huge wardrobe, except the handle was at the center of the unit toward the ground. It would have to open upward.

"Large, medium, small," Vince said, indicating the armor.

He frowned when his attention fell on me. "You might be a problem." He walked over to one of the pegs and grabbed a breast plate. He looked at me, and the breast plate, and nodded. "Should work."

"The chest over there contains skins," Hyde said. "One size fits all. You'll wear those under the armor."

Vince tapped the poster. "Use the guide and suit up."

The others around me were already busy stripping. I caught naked torsos and tight butts encased in boxers and then one or two glances were thrown my way.

"You gonna strip, Justice?" a cadet whose name I didn't know asked with a grin.

"Fuck off, Mal," Harmon growled, stepping in between the two of us.

"You boning her too, Harmon?" Mal asked with a sneer. "She's part of the team now, so surely we should all get a go?"

Harmon's hand curled into a fist, but like hell was I going to let him have the satisfaction. I stepped around him and planted my fist in Mal's face.

The cadet staggered back under the force of the blow. "Bitch." He leapt up and lunged but never made it, because Thomas had him in a headlock.

Hyde finally stepped forward. "Enough."

Heads jerked his way. Fuck, I'd forgotten he was in the room. Vince too. Neither had made a sound during the short altercation.

Thomas released Mal, and the guys glared at each

other, chests heaving. This one was going to be trouble. Carlo's warning filled my mind. I raked my gaze over the others. To be fair, most of them were looking daggers at Mal, and the rest just looked uncomfortable. Not all arseholes then.

"Bleedin' hell," Vince said. "You fuckers need to sort your shit out."

He advanced on Mal, but I didn't get to see what happened next because Hyde was steering me out of the room and into the corridor beyond. He shoved open the door to what looked like a broom closet and pushed me in.

"You can change in here," he said.

"A supply closet?"

"I'll get Vince to clear out a room for you to use while you're on duty here."

As much as a space of my own sounded great, it felt wrong. "I'll take a separate changing room, but I'll bunk down with my team, whoever that may be. I'm a shadow cadet, and I don't want to be segregated."

"You're also a woman amongst a bunch of horny supernatural males." He closed his eyes and exhaled through his nose as if he'd said too much.

But he had a valid point. "It's not like I have a choice, is it? If I isolate myself, I stay the shiny new thing. If I become one of the guys, then I lose the whole woman status and become a cadet. I become one of them."

His jaw flexed as he mulled this over. "Vince will be

here all the time. He lives here. So ..." It seemed like he was reassuring himself more than me. "I'll get your armor."

He left me in the closet and returned a moment later with a set of skins, breast and shoulder plates, and some shin pad things. "The greaves may be too big." He held out the bundle. "Vince will make you some armor to fit. You'll have it before the trial. In the meantime, you'll need to make do."

I took the armor. It was lighter than expected. And the reality of this situation hit me hard. This was my future, whether I liked it or not. I'd gone with the flow, neglected to dwell, to turn this over in my mind for what it was. My map. My goal. Chosen for me by fate.

This was a fighter's destiny, so why did my insides feel so twisted?

Doubt stabbed at my chest. What if I was shit at this? I'd learned to fight, to stand up for myself and not back down. I'd survived in the supernatural slums, but all I'd had to worry about back then was me. This was bigger than me. If I fucked up, other people could get hurt.

"Justice?"

I looked up and was caught in the snare of Master Hyde's gaze.

He sighed. "This has always been a male gig. Your being here is going to stir up shit. And yeah, it's going to take time for the others to accept you as an equal, to see you not as a woman but as a cadet. But you have just as much right to be here as they do." He pouted in thought. "I'll train you myself. One on one."

My gaze flew up to meet his. "Why would you do that?"

His smile was all sharp edges. "Because unlike those boys in that room, I won't go easy on you because you're a woman. I won't be trying to impress you to get in your pants."

My mouth was suddenly dry. The thought of him in my pants ...

Heat coiled in his blue-green eyes for a moment as if the same thought had just occurred to him too. He sucked in a sharp breath, and the heat evaporated.

"We start tomorrow. An hour before regular training. Are you in?" There was a challenge in his tone.

And despite my doubts as to the wisdom of being alone and sweaty with him, there was no way I'd back down from a challenge.

"I'm in."

SEVENTEEN

The skin fit like, well, like a skin. Swirling patterns decorated my legs where the almost see-through material clung. I hope they fucking washed these before getting us to wear them. They were so tight they were almost indecent. But then, if this was Winterlock Tech fabric, it was probably self-cleaning. The breast plate was a little too big, and the greaves were too long. It was like swimming in metal, but when I did move, the metal didn't clank together like I'd have expected. It molded to my limbs, not exactly but enough to not be totally awkward.

I joined the other cadets in the armor room. They were all suited up, and damn, did they look hardcore and impressive in the silver and black armor.

Hyde had slipped into armor too, and if he'd looked impressive before, he looked like a metal monolith now, one I'd have no problem climbing and then polishing with my body. I took a deep breath to dispel the inappropriate thoughts. Thank goodness Larkin wasn't about.

Hyde's gaze flicked my way, but his impassive expression didn't change.

"You okay, Justice?" Harmon asked.

"Yeah, just feeling ridiculous in this getup." The breast plate was too big and made it difficult for me to see my feet.

Harmon looked me up and down. "You look good to me."

His gaze was momentarily intense and very unHarmon like. "Um ... thanks?"

"Weapons," Vince said.

Hyde walked over to the closed unit and yanked on the door handle. The door slid up, folding into the wall to reveal too many pretties hung there: axes, swords, and huge hunting knives. It was an arsenal of stabby things.

"You'll be forging your own armaments next year," Vince said. "But for now, you'll be allocated a temporary weapon."

"Line up," Hyde ordered.

One by one, we approached Master Hyde, and one by one, he selected a weapon for us to wield.

"How come he gets to choose our weapon," someone behind me muttered.

"Cos he's the fucking master," Vince snapped. "Hyde knows weapons. He can gauge compatibility between wielder and weapon." Vince walked over and glared at the cadet who'd commented. "What do you think, Hyde? Is this one a short dagger guy?"

Hyde's eyes narrowed. "Maybe a bare fists kinda guy."

The cadet's eyes widened.

Vince let out a bark of laughter and slapped the guy on the back. "Don't worry. I'm sure you'll be fine."

The queue moved up, and it was my turn. Hyde stared at me for a long beat and then reached behind him and picked up a small axe.

Disconcerted mutters rose up behind me as Hyde handed me the weapon. Our fingers brushed as I grasped the hilt, and a zing of awareness shot up my arm. He froze for a fraction of a second. Had he felt it too? I looked up at him, but he seemed unaffected. He released the axe, and the weight settled in my hand.

"Try it," he said.

I stepped away from the line of cadets and turned my wrist, making figure eights with the weapon. I swung my arm so the figure eight grew larger. The whoosh of the blade cutting through the air felt right. The motion and weight perfectly balanced.

Several gasps and exclamations filled the air.

I nodded at Hyde. "This will do fine."

He grinned and reached behind him and unhooked another one. "They go together."

I took the other axe and moved back, swinging them both in a way that created a barrier of blade around me. I'd used twin blades before, but this was my first time with twin axes.

"Fucking awesome," Harmon said.

"Show-off," Thomas's tone was good-natured.

The others watched in awe that had my blood heating with pride. I guess the hours of training and hard work that my father had dismissed were going to come in handy after all.

I smiled up at Hyde. "This can work."

He returned my smile before turning his attention to Harmon.

I caught Mal staring and bared my teeth at him. Yeah bitch, I will cut you and I can do it fast.

He looked away quickly.

Vince wandered over to me and handed me something small and round affixed to a strap. It looked like a watch, but it was a compass. He made to walk away.

"Wait."

He arched a querying brow. "Yes?"

"The Academy is south of the mist."

His mouth turned down. "Is that a question?"

I gave him a flat look. "Is it south of the mist?"

He sucked in his lips. "It is, indeed."

"And these barracks are south too?"

"Correct."

I nodded. "Thank you."

He handed out the rest of the watch compasses, but no one else spoke to him or asked him any questions.

Several minutes later, Hyde had wrapped up his weapons allocation, and we were ready. Harmon had an axe and Thomas twin hunting daggers. We strapped on holsters relevant to our weapons. Mine slipped on like a waistcoat, so the axes sat against my back. Harmon helped adjust the straps to make it fit, his huge hands working deftly as if he'd done this before. It made me wonder about his life with the pack. Did they use weapons like these? Why would they need to when they had fangs and claws?

And then Hyde was leading us out of the barracks and into the night. The mist hovered fifteen meters away, rising like a wall to greet us. Feet faltered as everyone took a moment to appreciate the magnitude of what was about to happen. We were doing this. We were going into the grey stuff that shrouded the land.

And then we were moving fast, headed right for the mist, then into the mist, and then it was closing around us. I gasped as it touched my skin, and then coughed as it filled my lungs.

Others around me were doing the same.

"Relax," Hyde said. "It can't hurt you. Breathe normally."

I closed my eyes and willed my pulse to relax. It was mist. Nothing more. My pulse calmed and I opened my eyes to a world that was muted and hazy. Visibility was reduced by about thirty percent, but it was nowhere near as thick as it looked from the outside. The air tasted different, too. The taste was familiar. What was it?

"Licorice." Harmon spat the word from beside me. "Fucking hate licorice."

"Stay together," Hyde said. "You stray, and you're on your own."

He strode off, vanishing into the mist. We jogged to catch up. Shadows to the left and right.

"AM posts." Hyde came to a halt by a thick metal post. A ladder was attached to it. He placed his hand on it. "You'll be trained on AM maintenance starting tomorrow. You'll be split into three groups and allocated a second-year troop to man barracks with once a week."

He led us away from the post, farther and farther away from the barracks. Deeper into the mist.

"How far does sector one stretch, sir?" one of the cadets asked.

"A mile north. And a mile east and west," Hyde said. "The width of the breach."

He angled his body east and continued walking. A low hum registered.

"Do you hear that?" I nudged Thomas.

"Yeah," he replied. "I think that's the mechanism of the posts."

They were poisoning the air against the fomorians, but it looked like the air had an effect on the terrain too. The earth was dry and dusty, and I had no idea how any creatures could possibly live here.

Hyde came to a halt again, and beyond him, through the mist, a dark, cavernous space was visible. It looked like the mouth to a cave. We got closer, and yes, it was definitely a cave.

Hyde turned to us. "These are the catacombs. This is where your first trial will take place. The mouth of this cave leads to the only entrance and exit to the catacombs beneath. It's sealed up now, but it will be opened in three weeks for you. You'll be sealed inside for eight hours. If you survive, you pass."

Sealed in ... That hardly sounded like a trial, unless ... "What's inside there? What are you going to seal us in with?"

His expression was stony. "Hounds. You'll be sealed in with hounds and their younglings."

A shiver of apprehension rushed up my spine. "You want us to kill them?"

He smirked. "Or be killed. Your choice."

Someone snickered. Tosser. Obviously hadn't thought shit through like I had. It was why I was so confused. The knights raised and trained hounds to work alongside them. Killing them was counterproductive.

"Isn't it a waste to kill the hounds that the knights use?"

His brows snapped down, and then his frown cleared. "I see your confusion. Allow me to clarify. The hounds in the catacombs aren't ours. They're not trained. They're feral, and they're fed meager amounts of meat once a month to keep them alive. They've procreated and built their home in these catacombs, and their numbers are culled once a year by the cadets in the shadow trial." He canted his head. "That's you, by the way. Ten of you and goodness knows how many of them."

Was that worry skipping across his brutal features?

"If you want to survive the trial, you need to train hard. You need to work as a team. You need to be ready to kill."

He stared us all down, one by one. With the mist swirling around us and the night pressing in on us, his words were an ominous premonition of impending death.

He smiled. "So, how about we start with a mini test. If you find your way back to the barracks on time, you might get some lunch."

He turned away and strode off into the mist, leaving us huddled in a group.

"Shit!"

"What the fuck?"

"Which way?"

Exclamations broke out, and this test suddenly made sense. Vince had handed out compasses, and no one, aside from me, had questioned it. Fucking idiots. What would they have done if I wasn't here? Would Hyde have come back for them?

"Hey!" I held up a hand. "We head south." I tapped

the compass on my wrist. "You guys do know how to read a compass, right?"

Mal threw a filthy look my way. "And why the fuck should we listen to you? You could be trying to get us lost."

"Not everyone, just you." I walked up to him. "Because you're an asshole. And assholes should always be left behind."

The cadet beside him let out a bark of laughter. "She's got that right, Mal."

"Fuck you, Gimble," Mal said. "No one cares what a bastardized fey thinks."

Gimble, a skinny, mousy-haired guy with a pronounced Adam's apple, looked as if he'd been slapped.

Bastardized fey was a slur used to refer to the feybloods who came from lesser blood lines. Lines not directly associated with Winterlock and Bourne, and only assholes used the term anymore.

"And what does that make you?" I narrowed my eyes at Mal. "What is he, Harmon?"

Harmon shrugged a huge shoulder. "Not legacy."

"Bastardized nightblood," Thomas said with a smirk.

Mal reddened. "You think you're special, Justice, cos you got a pussy *and* the fucking gene."

"At least I'm not *just* a pussy."

He advanced toward me. "Let me tell you somethi — ompf."

My knee connected with his balls, and he went down, clutching the only jewels he'd ever get to hold.

I turned to the rest of the cadets. "I'm fucking hungry. How about we get back and grab some grub?"

I checked my compass and then set off south. Harmon and Thomas fell into step on either side of me. If the rest of them wanted to hang about, then that was up to them, but I needed some O neg and an apple. Stat.

EIGHTEEN

Harmon and I peered in through the round window to the med bay. It was four hours until dawn. Classes were over for the day, and I'd been on my way to see Minnie when I'd bumped into Harmon.

He hadn't asked me to come with him, but fuck it, he'd looked like he could do with some support, plus he'd stood up for me against Mal at the barracks. I owed him. The lights were dim out in the main med bay area, but they were lit up in Lottie's private room. She was sitting up in bed, reading a book. She looked ... normal.

"She's doing fine," Madam Mariana said from behind us. "Physically, of course, but I was unable to find any traces of her memories when I did a sweep of her mind. She's retained all her skills: reading, writing, and general knowledge is sound. But memories of attachments, childhood, family ... They all seem to be gone."

I turned away from the door. "What could cause this?"

"I don't know," Madam Mariana said. "Her temperature was elevated when she was brought in—a slight fever—which leads me to postulate that this could be the result of some kind of virus."

"Supernaturals don't get sick," Harmon said shortly.

"Not unless the sickness is supernatural in nature," Mariana added.

"A supernatural sickness?" I raised both brows. "Do we even have any? I've never heard of them."

Madam Mariana looked uncomfortable. "It may not be from our world."

Wait, was she suggesting ... "An Otherworld sickness?" Oh, shit. "You think it's fomorian?"

"An attack?" Harmon was on high alert now, his huge body bristling with the need to act.

I touched his wrist lightly, and he exhaled sharply. "Tell me about this virus?"

The weaver held up her hands. "It's just one theory. We can't say anything for sure. Unfortunately, there is no trace of antigen in Lottie's blood. Nothing for us to go on aside from speculation." She sighed. "She could be infectious, but then again, she may not be. My tests have picked up nothing conclusive. We have her in quarantine as a precaution. Master Payne is running more bloodwork as we speak. If all the tests are clear, she'll be able to go back to classes at the end of the week."

"My father ... Did you call him?" Harmon asked.

"I believe he was informed," Mariana said softly. "I'm sorry. He said he was too busy to come."

Harmon nodded. "Figures." He tucked in his chin. "Can I see her? Once the quarantine is over?"

"Of course." Mariana placed a hand on Harmon's shoulder, her expression flooded with sympathy. "She understands what's happened. She knows she has a brother here, family. She's much calmer now, and who knows, maybe seeing you will jog something."

The door to the lab opposite the reception area opened, and Master Payne strode in. "Everything okay?" His attention was on me before he glanced to the quarantine room. "How is the patient?"

"She's fine," Madam Mariana said. "We didn't mean to interrupt your work."

He shook his head. "No, that's fine. I'm coming up empty." He frowned. "I'm sorry this happened, Harmon. If there is a way to fix it, we will."

"Thank you," Harmon said.

Payne gave me a tight smile. "Are you settling in with the shadow cadets all right?"

"It's fine."

"Good." He cleared his throat, and there was an awkward silence.

Madam Mariana broke it with a deep sigh. She steered us from the room and closed the door on us.

Time was up, I guess.

"How can this happen?" Harmon said softly. "How can they not know anything?"

Shit happened, though. It happened all the time, and sometimes there was no rhyme or reason to it, and the only thing that kept us going was hope.

"You heard what Madam said. Maybe seeing you will jog something. Just because she can't remember now doesn't mean she won't."

"Yeah." Harmon smiled, but it didn't touch his eyes. "I never thought I'd say this, but you're right."

I snorted. "I never thought you'd stand up for me, but you did."

He ducked his head. "Yeah, well, Mal's a wanker."

Nah, it was more than that. It was about Harmon being a decent guy, despite his dickhead player façade.

"It'll be okay." I patted his taut bicep.

"Yeah. It will."

We parted ways, and I headed to Minnie's dorms. I'd said what I needed to make him feel better, but the whole virus shtick felt wrong. I mean, how did that explain the blood we'd found or the fact that Lottie's shoe had been discovered in the gardens and her body in the hothouse?

MINNIE GREETED me with a hug and then yanked me into her room. The familiar scent of her raspberry shampoo hit me. The room looked different. My side anyway. Bed stripped. Books gone. Dead.

"Bloody hell, did you hear?" she said.

I focused on her eager face. "Huh?"

"About Lottie."

"Yeah. I was just at the med bay with Harmon."

She blinked up at me in surprise. "You and Harmon are hanging out now?"

Were we? "No. Yes. I mean the cadet thing means we kinda have to."

"And how is that going?" She flopped down on her bed and crossed her legs in the familiar *let's gossip* pose.

"Um ... good."

"That's it?"

What could I tell her without breaking the oath? Not much. "I can't really talk about it."

She sighed. "Yeah, I figured." She gnawed on her bottom lip. "But are you okay? I mean, how is your room, and the other guys ... Are they accepting you?"

"There've been a few issues, but your brother was actually nice to me."

She mock gasped and clutched her chest. "No! Lloyd?" Then she grinned. "He can be an ass, but he's not an idiot. If you have the mark, then you're one of them. He'll treat you with respect."

"What about you? How's the studying going?"

"Urgh. I have literally spent every spare moment in

my library nook. I have it all set up for study. Books and notepad and pens, and so far, no one has touched my stuff." Her expression sobered. "What about you. You have a test coming up too, right?"

She must know some stuff from Lloyd's first year. "Yeah. In three weeks."

"I remember Lloyd was super tense before that one. I figured it wasn't a written test."

"No. No, it isn't."

We lapsed into silence for several long beats.

She blew out a breath. "I fucking hate that there's this whole part of your life I'll know nothing about now."

"It doesn't matter." Did it? "We have shit loads of other stuff to bond over." Didn't we?

"Yeah, course we do." She smiled weakly.

Two days ... it had barely been two days, and we were already lapsing into uncomfortable silences.

"Ooo." Minnie bounced on the bed. "Did you hear about Oberon?"

"No."

"He's gone. His family sent for him. Rumor has it his mother wasn't entirely faithful, and Oberon isn't a Hyde by blood. It's super rare for a Hyde not to get the mark, so I guess that's what tipped them off. In fact." She frowned in thought. "I can't recall a Hyde who's been sent to the Academy that hasn't ended up with the mark. They didn't all take up the shadow knight mantle back then, of course, but they got marked."

"Yeah, no conscription back then."

"Yeah."

We fell into silence again, but then the shrill ring of a bell had us both jumping, and a voice filled the room. My gaze shot up to the speaker fitted high up on the wall. An old Tannoy system.

"All students, please return to your dorm rooms immediately," Brunner said. "All students, please return to your dorm rooms immediately. This is not a drill."

I headed for the door, and Minnie made to follow me out.

I gently pushed her back into her room. "No, stay here. You heard what Brunner said. I'll see you later if possible. If not, I'll catch you at lunch tomorrow."

She looked like she wanted to argue, but Brunner's voice blasted through the Tannoy again. "All students, head back to your dorm rooms immediately, this is not a drill."

"Urgh. Fine. Be careful," she said.

I nodded and headed out into the dimly lit corridors.

TEN FIRST-YEARS and thirty second-years were squished together in the lounge, which felt way too small. Lloyd and his troop had congregated by the kitchenette; the rest of the second-years had claimed the available seating, leaving us newbies clustered by the door.

Larkin slipped between us, tail switching, eyes scanning each face. Finally, he leapt onto the table and stood, legs shoulder-width apart and arms crossed over his chest. He was dressed in a maroon velvet waistcoat, cream shirt, and black cargo pants today. It was an odd combination, but he made it work with his undaunting confidence.

"All accounted for," he said. "Two troops are at the barracks. Good. Good. You're probably wondering why the urgency? Another student went missing an hour ago. However, I received word ten minutes ago that he's been found safe and sound and is now in the med bay."

The room erupted with variations of the same question—was this the same as the Lottie incident?

"Hush!" He held up his hands for quiet. "Yes. Yes. Memory loss. Yes, they are investigating, and even though no one asked, yes there is now a two a.m. curfew for all cadets, shadow and Nightwatch. Unless you are on barracks duty, you will be in your dorms by two a.m., no exceptions."

"What about the boy?" someone asked. "What's doing this?"

"Not our problem." Master Hyde entered the room, bringing his citrus fresh scent with him.

Do not inhale too deeply. Too late. Shit, he smelled good.

"Our focus must remain on the mist," Hyde said. "Newbies, you need to focus on preparing for your first trial." His gaze skimmed my face before moving on. "Leave the investigation of these incidents to the administration."

"They think it might be a virus," Harmon blurted out.

All eyes were on him now.

He shrugged. "Fomorian."

Larkin frowned. "Who told you that?"

"Madam Mariana mentioned it to Justice and me earlier."

Hyde looked from me to Harmon. I tried to catch his eye, but his gaze slipped away.

"An Otherworld virus." Larkin tapped his chin with a claw. "Ingenious."

"Bullshit."

I looked to the back of the room at the speaker.

Carlo shrugged. "If they wanted to take us out, they'd target the shadow cadets first. Make us sick and stop us patrolling. Why target Nightwatch cadets?"

He had a point.

"It isn't our problem," Master Hyde reiterated. "We have a job to do, and we need to focus on that. If shadow cadets start losing their memories, then we'll reassess. Until then, it's business as usual."

God, he could be cold.

Harmon muttered something under his breath that I didn't quite catch.

Master Hyde strode out of the room, and Larkin clapped his paws together. "As you were, cadets. As you were. Make sure to check your rotation for the next two weeks." He leapt off the table and vanished.

"This is bullshit," Harmon said. "We need to know how this student lost his memory, where he was found, and if he was hurt."

He was right. There wasn't nearly enough information. "I don't think it's a virus."

"Me either," Thomas said. "A virus doesn't explain why Lottie's shoe was found one place and her body in the other. It doesn't explain the blood and the signs of struggle."

I agreed with all of this. "We can pop to med bay tomorrow and speak to the nurse. Find out what happened to the second victim."

The guys nodded.

The lounge was emptying out, but Lloyd loitered.

"Hey, Justice," he called out.

I looked over. "You and your friends are on barracks one duty with us next week." He jerked his head toward the notice board on the other side of the room. A white sheet of paper was pinned to it. "Rota is up." He followed his troop out of the lounge.

"We better get some rest," Thomas said. "Only thirteen days until the trial."

He and Harmon left for bed, and I headed out of the lounge toward the master quarters.

Although nightbloods didn't need as much sleep as

regular supernaturals, I'd always reveled in it. Besides, being awake during the day while everyone else slept didn't appeal. The extra sleep would come in handy because I had a one-on-one session with Hyde at sunset, and for some reason, I was eager to impress.

NINETEEN

O omf. I body-slammed the ground for the fifth time.

"Up," Hyde ordered.

Shit. I shook myself off and leapt to my feet, fists up, ready to defend.

"No." He shook his head. "Attack."

Fuck. I lunged. He blocked and then slammed a palm into my chest, sending me flying backward in some kind of move from a martial arts movie. Damn, any minute now, he'd leap up and start running in the air or something.

I rubbed my breastbone, shooting him a disgruntled glare and earning a slight smirk in response.

The fucker was enjoying this.

Losing was not in my nature. It wasn't in my DNA, and it wasn't happening today.

Not a competition.

Training.

Fuck you, inner voice of reason.

He hadn't been kidding about not holding back. Dried blood coated the back of my hands and crusted my lips from where he'd landed a punch to my face. Thank God I healed fast, but damn, it had hurt. Twenty minutes of being thrown around was starting to bruise my ego.

We'd met at sundown. No breakfast or shower yet. Official training started in two hours, and I hadn't succeeded in landing a hit yet.

Yeah, he wasn't messing about, and now he was studying me with his head canted to the side.

"You fight with passion," he said. "But you're rash in your moves. You've been lucky with your opponents thus far."

"Thus far? Who says thus far?"

He shrugged while I reveled in the sting of his words.

"I've fought some hardcore fighters."

"A-huh." He smirked. "In the pits?"

"Yes, in the pits. It's brutal in there." I sniffed. "Not like you'd know, *Hyde*. Legacy feybloods have it easy."

The smirk vanished. "You think so? You think being a Hyde means I had it easy?" His eyes were chips of flint in his face. "Being a Hyde comes with expectations, and we're trained hard from infancy to ensure we meet those expectations."

"Aw, did you have a tutor come to your house?" I fluttered my lashes, mouth turned down. "Must have been sooo hard for you."

"And yet you haven't been able to knock me down once."

I threw up my hands. "I'm not an arrogant idiot. You're a fucking shadow knight. I mean, how long have you been doing this? Nine, ten years?"

"Six," he said. "And three of them have been as a tutor."

What? "Wait ... How old are you?"

"Twenty-five." He looked away. "I graduated at nineteen and served for three years before .... Before taking the tutor role."

"Nineteen? Wait, you were Trial Master. How can a nineteen-year-old be Trial Master?"

His eyes narrowed. "You want to know my story? I'll make you a deal. Knock me down, and I'll answer your questions."

Adrenaline rushed through my limbs. Now that was motivation. "Deal."

He fell into a defensive stance. "This is the trial, and I'm a hound. Take me out, Justice."

He charged.

I spun and dodged his attack. He was a tank, but he was also light on his feet. A lethal combination. It didn't take him long to be on my tail again, and fuck, I was running from him in blur speed. I doubled back to get behind him and deliver a kick to his back that should have sent him sprawling but simply knocked him forward several paces. And then he was spinning to face me, arm shooting out to snag me out of the air as I attempted to blur past him. I went down but rolled away before he could pin me. His hand almost snagged my ankle, and there was only one thought in my mind as I ran for the shadows. I needed to get away, to put some distance between us.

A tingle ran through my body, and then the world went black. Moonlight bloomed, and I was back. But not in the training arena. I was standing outside the hothouse under a rapidly rising moon.

What the fuck had just happened?

MASTER HYDE WAS STANDING, arms loose at his sides, staring at the spot I'd run at with a dazed expression when I got back to the training arena.

He turned to face me. "Where did you go?" His tone was wary.

"I ... I came out at the hothouse. I mean ... everything went black, and then I was just ... there."

He walked slowly toward me as if approaching a skittish animal. My pulse sped up as he got closer. His sweat mingled with the citrus scent to create an aroma that was pure sex. It washed over me, soothing the panic at what had just happened and replacing it with the distracting heat of desire.

I took a step back and clenched my fists. Fuck, I did not trust myself to jump him right now.

He came to a halt a few feet away. "Have you been able to do *that* before?"

"What? No." My voice came out thicker. Shit, Justice. Focus on the weird teleport thing. God. "I don't even know what *that* was."

He rubbed his bottom lip with his index finger, drawing my eyes to his mouth. "Your genesis isn't exactly a conventional one. Leave it with me. In the meantime, keep your newfound ability to yourself."

"Why?"

"Trust me, being special can often end up biting you in the ass. You've got enough on your plate right now as it is."

His tone was reflective, the gruff edges somewhat softened.

"You sound like you speak from experience."

"You don't get to be Trial Master at the age of twenty without special skills."

Okay, now I was even more intrigued. "What kind of special skills?"

There was an amused twinkle in his eyes now, and oh, God, was that a slight smile to accompany it? My heart beat a little faster, and heat bloomed in my chest and up over my collarbones.

"Uh-uh." He wagged a finger at me. "You need to knock me down before I reveal my secrets." He grabbed his sword holster off the ground and strapped it to his slender hips.

His biceps flexed through the thin material of his shirt as he worked, and I took a moment to appreciate his form. The deep V of his shirt offered a glimpse of his hard pectorals and molded to his body like a second skin, lovingly caressing his eight-pack.

"Justice?" His baritone teased my senses.

I snapped my attention to his face, need brimming in my eyes. He sucked in a breath as our gazes collided. His lips parted, and his eyes churned with an indecipherable emotion.

We remained locked like that for long seconds in which every ounce of my will urged me to bridge the gap between us. To touch him. To taste him, and the way he was looking at me screamed that he wanted it too.

He broke eye contact first, his jaw hardening. "Go grab a shower and some breakfast. Official training starts in an hour."

TWENTY

A five-minute shower and I was hovering outside the Nightwatch dining room. The clink of cutlery and the hum of conversation swelled to fill the large space. I'd barely had a chance to speak to Minnie last night. If I could grab a half hour now ...

I spotted her when a tinkling laugh drew my attention across the crowded room.

Harper Bourne—golden-haired, bubble-gum-lipsticked Harper.

Laughing.

And sitting opposite her, with her back to me, was Minnie. Minnie must have said something funny because Harper laughed again, eyes twinkling. A hot needle stabbed at my chest, and my breath caught.

Damn.

Is this how Harper felt when she'd seen me and Minnie together?

It was at that moment that Harper glanced up. Her gaze locked with mine. I raised a hand in greeting, but she was already looking away, back to Minnie—smiling and nodding and continuing the conversation as if I wasn't even there.

And maybe I wasn't. Maybe I shouldn't be.

I was a shadow cadet now. I couldn't be there for Minnie, not like Harper could.

I turned and walked out of the dining room.

I had training to go to.

DESPITE MY BEST INTENTIONS, I found myself swinging by the med bay. Maybe I could get some info on the second victim? Maybe I just needed a mental distraction. I stepped onto the foyer and peered into the quarantine room. Lottie wasn't alone; a young man was sitting up in the bed beside her, and they were deep in conversation. He wasn't anyone I recognized, though.

Maybe Master Payne would have some answers. I went to knock on the lab door, but voices stalled me—male and female.

Payne and someone else ... Mariana?

She sounded upset.

I focused my nightblood hearing to listen in, but they must have been standing quite far from the doors because I could only catch snippets of the conversation.

"... You promised."

"I'm sorry ... last time ...."

"... trust you ... love you ..."

"Always. I would never ... love you."

Whoa ... I backed up from the door.

Well, that would explain why Madam Mariana had been so eager to get rid of Harmon and me the other day. She and Payne were a thing. I guess the tutors needed to get it on too.

My questions would need to wait for another day.

I left the lab, and this time didn't stop till I got back to the shadow cadet dorms.

THE DAY FLEW by as we trained in hand-to-hand combat and sword-to-sword, then it was back to barracks one for AM post repair training, followed by another trip to the mist where we were left to find our own way back, and finally, home for supper.

Home.

Weird how I'd been at Nightwatch for weeks and had never thought of it as home, but here, amongst the shadow cadets, my brain had finally flipped the belonging switch.

Maybe this was where I was meant to be, whether I liked it or not.

Harmon and Thomas were organizing a poker

game, and I'd been invited to the lounge, but my mind was restless. I'd avoided speaking to Minnie at breakfast and hadn't bothered to find her at lunch. Logic said it was the best course of action, that soon I'd be in the mist so often that there wouldn't be time to see her. Soon, I'd be a shadow knight, and she'd be out in the world, and what hope was there for our friendship then, but my heart ... My heart missed her and argued *fuck it. Live for the moment. Enjoy what you can now, dammit!*

And it was my heart that led me out of my dorms and into the Nightwatch Academy corridors at one-thirty a.m. with only a half hour till curfew.

Minnie answered the door in her favorite purple PJs clutching a romance novel to her chest.

"Indie?" She looked at her watch. "Shit." She pulled me into her room. "Are you crazy? You have fifteen minutes till curfew."

"I know. I just had to see you."

She closed the door behind me. "Is everything okay?"

Although I'd had no intention of telling her about spotting her earlier, the words just came out. "I came to breakfast this morning, saw you with Harper, and left."

She blinked at me. "Why didn't you come over?"

Good question. "Because I'm an idiot. I just thought, with the way things are now, with me and the shadow cadet shit, that I'll hardly see you anyway. That maybe it would be better to just step away and let you get back to the way things were before I came here."

"Indie. Harper and I—"

"I know. You guys were friends before, and you felt sorry for me, the loner, and you—"

"Whoa. I did *not* feel sorry for you." Minnie ran a hand over her face. "If anything, I was intrigued. Look ... truth is, I was in love with Harper, okay." She sat back on her bed with a *flumph* as if the admission had taken something out of her. "But Harper started dating this guy, and I was so mad and hurt, and then you came along, and it was the perfect way to get away from her. Make friends with you. Start afresh. Get over her." She peered up at me. "You understand?"

"Oh ..."

She reached for my hands and pulled me down to sit on the bed beside her. "Don't get me wrong. I love you to bits, and I'm so glad I took the leap to get to know you." Her eyes misted. "And I want us to continue to be friends, no matter what. It's easier to hang with Harper now that I'm over her is all."

Yeah, I didn't buy that. "Are you?"

"What?"

"Over her?"

She looked away.

I nudged her with my shoulder. "Crazy thought, but have you considered that she might feel the same way?"

Minnie's brows shot up. "What? You mean like have

feelings for *me*?" She shook her head and laughed. "No. Harper likes guys."

"Doesn't mean she can't like girls too."

Minnie's eyes narrowed, and she peered up at me from beneath her bangs. "What is it you're not telling me?"

Shit. It wasn't my place to say. "Nothing. Just, don't close off your heart too soon, okay?" I shrugged. "Give Harper a chance."

She looked wary, and then her gaze fell to the clock on the wall behind me. "Shit, Indie. It's two a.m."

Crap. "I'll be fine. To be honest, I don't see the point of the curfew. They don't even know what's caused Lottie's and the other guy's memory loss."

"The curfew makes the administration feel like they have some control. I heard that Brunner activated the Academy gargoyles. She has eyes and ears on the place now."

Urgh, gargoyles creeped me the fuck out. "I'll be careful."

I hugged her quick and then slipped out into the corridor.

Silence and gloom greeted me. The lights were low, and my boots sounded way too loud even though I was in sneak mode.

It was a long way between here and the shadow dorm. Look before you leap, Justice. Hyde had warned me to not act rashly during training, and here I was acting rashly in general. Maybe he was right.

Maybe I needed to stop and think things through more.

I was almost at the main staircase when a shadow climbed the wall—hulking with horns.

Gargoyle.

Dammit.

There was nowhere to run. Nowhere to hide except a pocket of shadow.

Shadow.

God, please let this work. Get me out of here. I leapt at the shadows as the gargoyle rounded the corner. A tingle ran over my skin, and the world went black. I took another step, and my boot snagged on something. I tumbled forward just as my vision returned. Hyde's shocked face greeted me. And then I was barreling into him, and we were falling. Legs tangled, noses bumped, and my breasts squished up against his taut, naked chest.

Oh, my God. I was lying on top of my half-naked tutor. In his room. On his bed and he had his hands on my hips. I should move. Push him away. Get off him. Something. But I was mesmerized by the gold flecks in his eyes and the thick lashes that framed them. His pupils dilated, showcasing my reflection—parted lips and heavy-lidded eyes.

If I moved, the spell would be broken. If I moved, then I wouldn't be touching him anymore. I wouldn't be able to feel the length of his powerful body against mine or feel the heat of his skin seeping through my clothes. And right now, that was all I wanted. Here in his room, surrounded by lamplight, anything felt possible. Our faces were so close that our breath kissed. It would be so easy to bridge the gap and press my mouth to his lips.

But he was my tutor and a feyblood. There was no future there, even though my body didn't care about that. My hands were on his biceps, and I pressed down with my fingertips, wanting to feel that velvety skin just for a moment before I broke contact.

He sucked in a breath, and his grip on my waist tightened. Heat spiraled inside me, shooting down to my core.

"Indigo ..." One word filled with torment.

But fuck, he'd said my name.

He closed his eyes as if in pain. "You need to get up now." His voice was hoarse.

Oh, shit.

I pushed off him, and my thigh grazed something hard and long. And ... Oh, man ... was that ....

"Shit." He slid out from under me so fast I fell face first onto his bed.

I sat up to find him standing, hands on hips, with his back to me. The scars that crisscrossed his back stood out starkly in the lamplight.

"Fucking hell, Justice, what the hell are you doing here?"

My mouth refused to work for a moment, too dry. I licked my lips and took a much needed breath. "I went to see my friend in the Nightwatch dorms and got caught outside of curfew, and I ... I did that thing again. I shadow phased."

His shoulders rose and fell, and then he walked over to his dresser, grabbed a white tee, and pulled it on.

"And it brought you here? To my room?" He turned to face me, his expression pissed. "Do you know what will happen to me if anyone catches you in my room?"

Nothing good, that was for sure. "I'm sorry. I didn't do it on purpose. I wanted to get away from the gargoyle, and I just leapt into a patch of shadow."

"That doesn't explain why it brought you here." He crossed his arms. "Were you ..." He cleared his throat and looked at the floor. "Were you thinking about me?"

Had I been? Oh, God. "Yes! Just before it happened, I was thinking how you might be right about me being rash, and then I was here."

"I see. So, you can control it. You just need to focus." He sucked his bottom lip into his mouth. "Try it now. Go from that patch of shadow to the one across the room."

I'd expected him to kick me out, but it looked like he wanted to train me. "Um. Okay." I focused on the shadows—on the patch I was about to leap into—and visualized the other side of the room.

I ran forward, into the tingle that took over my body. The darkness enveloped me, and then the room materialized, but I was seeing it from a different angle as I stepped out from the other side of the room.

"Intent helps," he said. "But I'm guessing you have to be focusing on a person or a place for it to be accurate or you could end up anywhere."

He walked toward me and placed his hands on my shoulders. That close, he was a head and a half taller than me, and my eyes were level with his pecs. I looked up into his beautifully scarred face. This close I could smell him, that fucking citrus aroma that made me want to lick him.

"Now," he said, his voice low and intimate. "Do you think you can shadow phase yourself to your own room?"

SLEEP REFUSED TO COME. I'd shadow phased into Hyde's room and felt him up. I'd given him a boner. Unless ... Wait, had that already been there?

Urgh.

I needed to shut off my brain and sleep.

Long minutes ticked by.

Not happening.

Sod this. I threw back the covers, shoved on my slippers, and headed out of my room to the lounge.

It was dark and empty, but the dark didn't bother me. My night vision was excellent. Maybe a bag of warm blood would help. They kept A positive in the fridge, and there was a microwave here too. Whoop de do.

I prepared my drink and curled up on the sofa with it.

The hairs on the back of my neck stood to attention.

"Can't sleep or won't sleep?" Larkin asked. He materialized slowly like a polaroid picture, perched on the sofa opposite me. "Oh, look, you didn't even jump. The guys yelp." He grinned. "Every time."

Even though the hour was late, he was still immaculately dressed in a silver waistcoat and navy-blue trousers. His hair was brushed forward over the stripes on his forehead, and his eyes glowed in the dark like tiny slanted lamps.

I finished off the blood and licked my lips. "I'm not a yelper."

"No? But you're a visit-her-tutor-in-his-room-in-the-middle-of-the-night kind of woman, aren't you?"

He blinked, and his pupils widened. The atmosphere went from playful to menacing.

Panic gripped my chest. "It's not like that. It was an accident."

"You *accidentally* walked into his room?" He tapped his chin with a claw. "Let me see. Oh, Principal Brunner, I *accidentally* walked into Master Hyde's bedroom and then stayed in there for a good ten minutes."

Annoyance mingled with the panic swirling in my chest. "You were spying on us?"

"It's my job to keep watch on the occupants of this dorm." Larkin's drawl was less relaxed now. "Now, tell me why I shouldn't report you?"

This was what Hyde had been worried about. I couldn't let Larkin report us. I was the student. I'd get a slap on the wrist, but Hyde ... Hyde could lose his job. His place here. Oh, shit.

"Fine. The truth is that I phased into his room by accident. It's a thing I can do. I broke curfew and had to get back quickly, but I got my location mixed up and ended up in Hyde's room."

He blinked slowly at me. "Oh."

"Oh?"

"I thought you were going to say you were in love with him or something, which would be fine. I mean, the hunk of a man deserves some action, and the way the administration has treated him ... *pffft*, fuck them. But I like your version better." He slid off the sofa in a catlike, sinuous way and sidled up to me. "Tell me about this shadow phasing."

I filled him in on the training incident and then the curfew and how I'd ended up in Hyde's room.

"How exciting. What did Brunner have to say?"

I winced. "Yeah, I'm not telling her. I just ... I want to get a grip on it first. To understand it. I mean ... I'm a nightblood female with a shadow knight gene and now this weird ability? I need to get my head around it."

"Hmmmm." Larkin moved closer, his eyes huge and compelling. "Yes, you certainly are a nightblood, but more ... so much more."

I shuffled away from him. "Has anyone ever told you, you have issues with personal space?"

"I have no problem with personal space." He grinned. "I love it. It's Hyde who has issues. The man has been alone for too long. Doesn't even take portal leave to stick it to the ladies."

Oh, God. "Are you seriously having this conversation with me?"

"I don't know? Am I? Or maybe you're asleep, and all this is a dream, in which case you can ask me anything, and I would be compelled to answer."

I had no idea what game he was playing, but like hell was I going to pass up the opportunity to find out more about Hyde.

"What happened to Hyde. How did he lose his leg?"

Larkin gave me a sly look. "Surely this is a question you should be asking him."

"Probably, but I'm asking you."

He considered for a moment and then shrugged. "It got eaten, just like they say. Snapped right off in the mist when he was hunting for hounds. Came as a shock it did, considering they called him the hound whisperer. It was his special skill. Hyde could mesmerize a hound and bring it down easily. It was why he got the gig of Trial Master in the first place. But something went wrong that fateful day."

"Wait ... so, he didn't carry someone back while missing a leg?"

Larkin stared at me. "Are you listening to yourself?"

Okay. He had a point, that sounded ridiculous.

"Redmond found him when he didn't return to the barracks," Larkin said. "He carried him back, bleeding and unconscious."

"And the scars on Hyde's back?"

Larkin smirked. "Those came way before. Courtesy of the Hyde family, and that *is* Archer's story to tell."

Was that what Hyde had meant when he'd mentioned the training Hydes went through. This was why Oberon had been so devastated when he didn't get the mark. He'd said he'd failed. It was obvious the Hyde family put a lot of emphasis on becoming a shadow knight.

I focused on Larkin's face. "The Watch gave Redmond Hyde's job."

"To be fair, the job was meant to go to Redmond before Hyde revealed his hound whisperer trick. Trial Master means a nice retirement package, a house, and generous annual income for doing absolutely fuck all. But yes, that is correct. Hyde was a prodigy. A legend. A master. And then he was just a tutor. But he's a fucking great one, and you'd be lucky to have him."

Why did I feel like there was a double-entendre there?

"Because there is." Larkin winked and then vanished.

Fuck.

I would need to watch what I thought when he was around. I needed to watch myself when Hyde was around too, because the more time I spent around him, the closer I wanted to get to him.

It was dangerous. For both of us. But tomorrow was a new day. Tomorrow my focus would be entirely on training. I'd lost out on too much. Parents who loved me. Freedom of choice when it came to my life, and quality time with my best friend. The only thing I had left, the only thing I had control over, was how kick-ass I could be at this shadow cadet shit. And there was no way I'd start off by losing the trial.

TWENTY-ONE

P erspiration beaded my brow, and my hands shook as I reached for the component.

"Come on, Justice," a smooth baritone drawled. "I haven't got all day."

"Fuck you, Aidan."

The mist swirled around me, a chill swept across my skin, and my knees trembled while my boots remained firmly locked onto the ladder of the AM post.

I'd taken off the casing easily this time. Checked all the wires and connections, which meant the problem was the snap component—not the technical name for it, I'm sure, but it's what the guys called it because ... I grasped the tiny piece of feytech between index finger and thumb and tugged.

Snap.

That's why.

"Oh, for fuck's sake. Again?" Aidan's voice echoed around me.

I closed my eyes, tamping down on my agitation, and then looked up into the simulated sky. "You know, this would be so much more realistic if you shut the fuck up."

Laughter warm like honey surrounded me. "What and leave you all alone in the wastelands with your clumsy, fat fingers?"

"I do not have fat fingers."

"Try again." The humor bled from his tone.

I visualized his handsome, stubbled face, his warm hazel eyes and the mouth that turned up slightly at the corners as if he was always on the verge of smiling, and then planted an imaginary fist in it.

The simulation reset, and there it was again—the faulty conductor box. I ran through the steps once more until I got to the part where I needed to pull out the snap. It was a tiny rectangular component lodged lengthwise into the box and gripped tightly by metallic claws. Sixth time's the charm, maybe? I took a deep breath, and then carefully flicked one edge of the snap upward. It came free easily. Oh, okay. I gripped and slid it out.

Bingo.

"Ha! In your face, Aidan."

"Aidan got bored and went to make a sandwich." This voice was grumblier but just as smooth.

Devon, Aidan's twin.

"Fuck the sim," he said. "Grab a bite to eat, and I'll take you out to deal with the real thing."

The world went black, and then I was looking up into Devon's face. His eyes were hazel like his brother's, but whereas Aidan had more gold in his eyes, Devon's were streaked with emerald. His mouth was poutier than Aidan's, and his hair was cut shorter, killing the wave that gave Aidan his playful look. Devon looked like he meant business. He hauled me out of the sim pod with a frown.

"You want to learn, then you need to get out there."

"I know that, but your brother insisted I needed to run the sim with one hundred percent accuracy first."

Devon tapped the monitor, which depicted my stats. "You nailed it every time. Aidan manipulated the results." He exhaled through his nose. "He hates training newbies."

"What? Wanker!"

Devon smiled. "He can be."

"And you? You don't mind training newbies?"

He levelled a look at me that was hard to read. "I think of it as a mini vacation."

There was darkness in his hazel eyes now, swirling around like a mini vortex. He blinked, and it was gone. My imagination?

"Go get fueled up," he said. "You head out into the mist in half an hour."

THE KITCHEN WAS SANDWICH CENTRAL. Aidan was already stuffing his face with what looked like a triple decker ham, cheese, and sausage concoction, while Carlo sawed at a huge loaf of bread and Thomas slathered it with butter. Lettuce and tomato and various meats were piled on the counter.

I glanced over Thomas's shoulder. "Since when do you care about sandwiches?"

"Since my allocated mentor told me I did," Thomas said with a smile.

Carlo raised the bread knife in the air and twirled it. "I do have a particular skill when it comes to sandwich concoction."

"You're a nightblood. We don't eat for pleasure."

"Speak for yourself," he snorted. "Life is nothing without a variety of flavor. Plus, I like figuring out what'll make other people go *mmmm*." He fixed his gaze on me. "If you know what I mean?"

"Are you going to be the innuendo guy of the group?"

"Well, I'm certainly not Mr. Strong and Silent Type."

Brady walked into the room with his signature fuck-off face on.

"Oh, there he is," Carlo said cheerfully. "Mr. I'll Crush Your Skull for Breakfast."

"Fuck off." Brady slumped down in the two-seater sofa by the window. "Dead out there. Nice."

"Right?" Carlo sighed happily. "I fucking love sector one."

Harmon strode in, covered head to foot in some kind of green goo. He stood in the doorway and glared at Brady.

"Apart from the dying critter we came across," Brady said.

Wait, was that a hint of a smirk on the monolith's face?

Everyone stopped what they were doing to stare at the moonkissed.

"You call that little?" Harmon was fuming. "You call that dying?"

Brady's expression hardened; he was out of his seat and in Harmon's face in an instant. "Little. Dying. Yes."

To give him credit, Harmon barely flinched. He met the larger male's gaze head-on, and then the anger left his features, and his gaze fell to Brady's neck.

I noted the exact moment when the rage left him. His shoulders relaxed, and he nodded. "Okay. Thanks for clarifying that. I should go shower." He turned on his heel and vanished down the corridor to the shower room, no doubt.

Brady turned his back on Harmon and resumed his seat. "Beef and mustard," he growled.

"On it." Carlo set to work.

Brady and Aidan stood face to face, fists out.

"Rock, paper, scissors."

Brady threw rock, and Aidan threw paper.

"Fuck." Brady shot a withering glance my way.

Thomas leaned in. "Do you think they do this every time they need to decide who's going to take a cadet out?"

I swung my legs from the perch on the counter. "Hey, guys. I'm beginning to get a complex here."

Yeah, it looked like no one wanted to play mentor. My gaze went to the window, to the rolling mist, and something inside me tugged with the need to be inside it.

The door rumbled as it opened, and then boots echoed down the corridor. Vince and Lloyd entered a moment later. Lloyd's blond hair looked lank and in need of a wash, his eyes were bloodshot. He and Vince had been working sector two, something to do with an increased vigilance warning that had come down from the fortress.

"You bastards!" Vince exploded at the sight of Brady and Aidan in a face-off. "I told ya, no. No more fucking rock, paper, scissors. This ain't no fucking vacation."

Lloyd coughed into his hand ... or was he laughing. Not too sure. Brady and Aidan turned to give him a flat look.

"Who's up for a tour?" Lloyd asked.

"Justice," Devon said. "AM post training."

Lloyd nodded. "Fine, I'll do it."

"No." Brady stalked toward me. "I got this." He jerked his head in the direction of the armory. "Suit up."

"Now why the fuck didn't he just say that sooner?" Aidan's voice followed me down the corridor.

Brady threw my gear at me, and then stripped off his shirt, turning his back on me. A bronze expanse of smooth, taut flesh spanned his wide pectorals and tapered at his waist. He was ... perfect. I pulled my gaze up to snag on the angry scar that marred the side of his neck; it cut down to his collarbone, and for some reason, I was bridging the distance between us, mesmerized by the mark.

He tensed but held his ground. His dark gaze was wary and questioning, so unlike the Brady I'd seen so far, but then his expression hardened.

"You want to know how I got this?" He touched the scarred flesh. His brows came together, and he canted his head. "Does it excite you, Justice?" He stepped closer, bringing the heat of his body with him, pushing it against mine.

My pulse was suddenly hammering too fast, blood fizzing in my veins. "There's nothing exciting about the wounds that skirt death. But I have a right to be curious." Why was my voice so breathless? I reached up on impulse, intent on touching the scar.

His hand shot up to grasp my wrist in a grip that was almost painful. "Don't."

Shit, what the fuck was I thinking? "I'm sorry. I … It's just that this … this could happen to me soon."

His chest rumbled, and then his fingers uncurled from around my wrist.

I dropped my hand to my side. Cheeks flaming. "I didn't mean to—"

"Get your armor on." He reached for the waistband of his joggers, preparing to tug them down, and for a moment, I was frozen in place, curiosity warring with modesty. "You gonna stay for the show?"

I turned and jogged for the closet.

IT WAS LATE. Brady and Devon were manning the control room, a place of blinking lights and schematics. A huge map of the sector covered one wall. It was dotted with green lights, which meant all was well.

Lloyd had explained that orange lights meant posts needed maintenance and red indicated the posts needed immediate repair. Vince was doing an armory audit or something equally mundane, and the rest of the cadets had scattered around the barracks doing whatever. These were the twilight hours between darkness and dawn when all was quiet and dead. I needed to shift my arse into the shower.

Nightbloods didn't need sleep, but my body begged to differ. My arms lay loosely at my sides, and my legs were splayed out in front of me, my ass almost slipping off the sofa. I'd sat down for a minute, and that had been twenty minutes ago. Brady had run me ragged. I mean, if I looked at my ass in the mirror, it probably wouldn't be there. Gone, because he'd worked it off. We'd walked miles and miles and climbed and climbed and replaced components and chased hairy critters, or so he said, but I hadn't seen anything. I swear he'd just wanted me to run.

A shadow fell over me. "Justice?"

I looked up at Lloyd. "I don't think I can move."

He rolled his lips into his mouth to bite back a smile. His blue eyes warmed with mirth. "Ah, the first timer crash. The mist has a different composition to regular air, and it can drain you, even nightbloods." He held out his hands. "Come on. Let me get you into bed."

"You wish." I took his hands though because fluffy pillows sounded sooo good right now.

He hauled me up, and I slumped against his chest. "Hold me."

He laughed and then scooped me off my feet. I wrapped my arms around his neck, surrendering the hard-ass act for a moment and reveling in being looked after.

"Shit, she okay?" Aidan asked as we entered the dorms.

"She's wiped."

"First timer crash?" Aidan whispered.

"Yeah."

I was lowered onto a soft mattress.

"You did good today, Justice," Lloyd whispered in my ear before releasing me.

Clouds cradled me, and then I was floating away.

TWENTY-TWO

Hyde pinned me to the ground, his weight settling over me and stealing my breath. Our legs tangled, limbs brushing and pressing together— the tautness of muscle and the unyielding hardness of metal.

A smile curved his lips. "Not this time, Justice."

He tightened his grip and angled his body so that it was impossible for me to flip him off me. Shit.

I struggled, my breath coming faster, part exertion, part excitement. Every inch of me was alive in that moment because he was touching me. He moved his leg, and his thigh rubbed against my crotch with delicious friction. Heat seared me, and a low, involuntary moan escaped my lips.

My ears burned with embarrassment at the same time as my mouth softened and swelled. Our gazes snagged, and he froze. I tried to pull it back, to hide the desire that floored me, but it was all over my face and rising off my body, which was pressed flush against his. There was no way he hadn't seen it.

He was off me quicker than a cat leaping off hot coals. Cool air washed over me, rushed into my lungs, and I gulped to clear my head and get my crazy libido under control. I needed blood. I needed to sink my fangs into something. I needed to fuck.

I rolled onto my side, chest heaving, and watched him walk stiffly to his holster and scoop it off the ground. He kept his back to me as he buckled it on.

"Good session." His voice was rough.

Okay, keep it light. Keep it neutral. "Maybe we can work on the parrying some more next time?" Shit, I sounded like I'd just run a marathon, all breathless.

I pulled myself up and brushed off my clothes.

"You're ready." He turned to face me. "Ready as you'll ever be. Only three more days left till the trial, and you have barracks duty tonight."

Where had the time gone? Two weeks had flown by in a blink.

He walked over to what I called our bench. It was the spot we hung out at after our sessions and before official training and barracks duty. Okay, so he wasn't going to run off. Good. I liked these chats. Maybe a little too much.

He sat forward, his arms braced on his thighs. "How are you settling in with Lloyd and his troop?"

"Good." I joined him. "I've learned a lot."

"I think your father would be proud of you."

Tension gripped my shoulders and the familiar flare of anger lit my chest. "I really don't give a shit what my father thinks."

He nodded slowly. "I can relate to feeling that way. But age and experience bring wisdom. I learned a long time ago that not caring was the easy choice." He spoke softly, almost as if he was sharing a secret. "Telling myself I didn't need his love or his pride made it stop hurting so bad when he dismissed me."

He was opening up, and suddenly, I was afraid to move or speak in case I shattered the moment. But he'd lapsed into silence, and I needed to speak, to prod him to tell me more.

I studied his profile. "What is it like? Back home for you? What's it like to be a Hyde?"

For a moment, I thought he wouldn't answer. That he'd shut down and dismiss me, but then he sat back, relaxing against the bench. One arm out so it draped on the wood behind me.

His gaze misted as if he was casting his mind back through time. "It's a wonderful honor. You're made to feel special. Prized. But it's also terrible because there is no room for failure. Ever. Being a Hyde is a trial that lasts a lifetime, and those that disappoint are cut off."

I wanted to ask about the scars on his back. I wanted to ask who hurt him, but the words stuck in my throat because in that moment he looked so sad and lost, and the urge to hold him, to wrap my arms around him and cradle him was a burning need radiating from my heart.

He understood me. Really got it, but he was out of my reach.

He turned his head to look at me, his blue-green eyes warm and open. "You may not have belonged at home, but you belong here. You can feel it, can't you?"

"I didn't ... not until I was marked. But being a shadow cadet feels right. Being here with you feels right."

I wanted to bite back the words as soon as they spilled from my lips. What was I doing? I might as well throw myself at him. Oh, wait, I'd already done that.

I waited for the shutters to come down. For him to slip into backup mode, but instead, his gaze roved across my face as if mapping every inch.

"I admire you, Indigo."

"You do?"

His lips tugged in a small smile, and his eyes hardened. "I admire your diligence and hard work. I'm fascinated by your abilities, and I want to know more. I'm honored to train you, but that is all. Do you understand me?"

A pit opened up inside me. A yawning pit of embarrassment and disappointment. He was gently letting down the student who had a crush on him. Me. That would be me. What the fuck had I expected? He was off limits. But over the past few weeks, he'd gotten under my skin and become a confidant. Despite my best intentions, I'd found myself slipping and falling for him, and here he was resetting the boundaries.

I felt sick. All the bravado, all the fight abandoned me, and I was just a woman who was yearning for a guy who was turning her down. Rejection hurt.

I ducked my head. "I understand."

"Good." He stood and looked down at me with an unfathomable expression. "Get back to the dorms."

He strode off, leaving me perched on the bench with an aching heart and ears burning with shame.

I WAS out in the mist during the day.

Again.

Sunlight never got old, even if it was filtering through fog. It kissed my cheeks and warmed my skin, and for the first time in forever, it didn't weaken my body.

"You'll get used to it," Lloyd said.

"I don't think I ever will."

"You have the shadow gene. You'll never be vulnerable during daylight again," he reminded me.

I could feel the power more acutely now. With my nightblood powers dormant, the shadow gene powers filled my veins with crackling heat. I could run, leap, fight. It was all still there, but it was shadow gene strength, not nightblood. It was strong, almost as if my nightblood power muted the shadow gene power.

227

Our boots scuffed the dried earth as we made our way back to the barracks in companionable silence. Who would have thought there'd ever have been anything companionable between me and Lloyd?

But Minnie had been right. He wasn't a total asshole like I'd thought. In fact, he was a pretty good stand-in mentor for Hyde. Sorry. *Master* Hyde.

It was important to make the distinction, to remind myself that he was off limits. He'd made that clear, and the memory of that conversation made me cringe internally.

I couldn't allow myself to fall for him. I needed to cut off those feelings and move on.

Lloyd and I had run maintenance on a couple of AM posts, done a sweep, and now it was time to head back and put our feet up for an hour or so.

I studied his profile—aquiline and strong. Being in sector one was a break for him and his troop. They never discussed sector two, or the trial they were working toward, and damn, it was hard not to ask about it. But the vibe around that subject was a clear back-off one.

I was content to fall into the routine we'd established over the last couple of weeks. Being at the barracks was like being in our own little world. It was beginning to feel like a home away from home. It was hard work, but it was paying off because I could fix an AM post in less than five minutes now, even though apparently that was still too long. Go figure.

Vince was doing some checks at another barracks in sector two, so it was just the troop and us newbies.

Lloyd had even allowed me into the inner sanctum of the control room.

Barracks shifts ran over a twenty-four-hour period, so we took turns to sleep. Being a nightblood, I didn't need as much sleep, so the twins Aidan and Devon, as well as Brady and Harmon were tucked up in their beds while Lloyd, Thomas, Carlo, and I manned the station during daylight hours.

"You're doing good," Lloyd said, slowing his pace slightly.

"Thanks." I slid a glance his way. "You sound surprised."

He smiled. "That probably sounds chauvinistic, but believe me, the fact you're a woman isn't why I'm surprised."

"Oh?" I had an inkling where this was going, but why make it easy on him?

He cleared his throat and kept his gaze on the misty terrain ahead. "You don't exactly come across as a hard worker. You skipped lessons, fell asleep in the ones you did attend, and were a bad influence on my sister."

My instinct was to jump into defensive mode, but I took a breath and mulled over his words. "First two, agreed. I didn't want to be here, and like fuck was I going to pay attention to shit that I found boring. But I did *not* influence your sister. Now that I think of it, *she* influenced *me*." I smiled. "If not for her, I don't think I'd have gone to *any* lessons."

He was silent for a long beat. "Point taken. But you do understand my reservations, right? You have a reputation for not giving a fuck."

Ouch, that hurt. More than it should have, because hadn't I gone out of my way to cultivate this exact image? I should be pleased I'd succeeded, but for some reason, the fact that he saw me that way pissed me off.

"I give a fuck when I want to. Nightwatch wasn't my choice. I was coerced and manipulated into being here. Not a great motivator."

"And outside? The fights? The living in the slums and rubbing your family's nose in it?"

"Wow, someone's done their research."

"Trust me, there was no research required. You were all they talked about at every social gathering. You know they call you the Fallen Justice."

Another bite into my ego. No wonder my father had been eager to frame me for murder. He wanted to get me under control—not for me but for the family reputation.

"Nice. Real nice. I might adopt that."

"No." He stopped and turned to face me. "Don't. That isn't who you are. Not anymore. I don't know what motivated you to be that person, but it's not the person I see."

My throat pinched. "What do you see?"

His icy-blue eyes warmed. "I see a woman that

gives a damn. I see a woman with heart. I see a fucking shadow knight in the making."

Damn him, and his words that had me all choked up, and when I got choked up, the defensive mechanism kicked in. Hard.

"Nope." I brushed past him and continued toward base.

"Nope?" He jogged and caught up. "What do you mean, nope? I just complimented you."

"You're not supposed to compliment me. You're supposed to be an arsehole. Faraday, the stick-in-the-mud."

He chuckled. "Is that what you think of me?"

"That is what *we* call you behind your back."

"We?"

"Oh, yes, in *my* social circles." I flicked my gaze to his face then back to the mist.

A smile flirted on his lips.

Flirted.

Was this flirting?

The back of my neck grew warm. Fuck this fluttery feeling. "Hey, Faraday. Last one back to base cooks supper."

And I was off.

TWENTY-THREE

"What you thinking, Justice?" Carlo asked. "You thinking how you're gonna lose?"

I held my cards close to my chest. "Nah, just how I'll enjoy watching you cry when *you* lose."

Thomas laid his cards on the table. "You can both cry, bitches."

Damn, he had a straight flush.

Lloyd pouted and studied Thomas's hand. "Nice. But not good enough." He laid down a royal flush. "I win. Again."

"This would be more fun if we were playing for money," Carlo said.

He tugged on a lock of his sandy hair and then raked his hand through it and slumped back in his seat.

We'd pulled a table from the whiteboard room and set chairs around it. No one liked sitting at the bench table. This way, the guys could sit with their legs splayed and let their balls breathe.

The door to the kitchen opened, and the twins Aidan and Devon ambled in half naked and scratching the backs of their heads. Devon was wide and powerfully built—all muscle—and Aidan was slimmer, but every inch of his torso was toned, hard muscle that rippled when he moved.

Whoa. Was it getting hot in here? I fixed my eyes on my cards even though the game was over.

"Guys, ever heard of T-shirts?" Carlo asked.

"And deny Justice the view?" Aidan winked at me good-naturedly.

Devon mumbled something and headed for the coffee pot.

Brady entered the room next, dressed but barefoot. He didn't speak, didn't even look at anyone, but headed straight to the coffee pot where Devon was ready with a steaming mug of coffee.

Brady took it and glugged it down and then held it out for a refill.

Yep. This troop was a well-oiled machine.

"WHAT DID WE MISS?" Harmon asked as he joined us. He looked freshly showered, but his eyes were bloodshot. "Anything on the monitors?"

Like me, Harmon had thrown himself into every shadow cadet task. It was a distraction from the fact that his sister no longer knew him. He made a point of seeking her out, of spending time with her, but every time he returned, he looked like he'd been punched in the gut. It was obvious things weren't going too well.

"Just patrols," Lloyd said. "Standard shit." He pushed back his seat, stood, and stretched. "Brady, you okay to take point?"

Brady grunted.

That obviously meant yes.

"In that case, I'm going to lie down for a couple of hours." Lloyd looked to the other nightbloods. "You guys can get some shut-eye too if you want."

Thomas gave Harmon a questioning look, but the moonkissed's attention was on his java.

Things had been strained between those two. I'd stayed out of it, but the look of pain that flitted across Thomas's face at Harmon's disinterest made my heart ache for him. If they'd been regular Nightwatch cadets, then I'd have said best to nip this in the bud—there was no future for them outside of here. But they were shadow cadets. If we survived, this would be our home for the next twenty years. There was no reason for them not to be together.

"I guess I'll grab some rest," Thomas finally said. He glanced at Harmon one more time, but the moonkissed merely nodded and sipped his coffee.

Ouch.

Thomas headed to the dorm.

Carlo stretched. "Yep. I'll take that lie-down. What

about you, Justice? Want to come snuggle?" He wiggled his eyebrows.

I smiled sweetly and fluttered my lashes. "I can snuggle my fist in your face?"

He let out a bark of laughter. "She loves O neg. She curses like a dude, and she doesn't take my shit. I've found my perfect nightblood, and she's totally friend zoned me."

I resisted the urge to muss up his blond hair. He was brash and loud, but he was fucking adorable. But like hell would I tell him I thought that. He blew me a kiss and headed out of the room.

Brady fixed his dark eyes on me. "If you're staying up, take control room duty with Harmon." He drained his mug. "Devon and Aidan, do a run."

Devon stretched, leaning his head from side to side to loosen his muscles. "I could do with a run."

It took a moment to click that they meant in wolf form. I hadn't seen their wolves before. Harmon looked torn, like he wanted to join them.

"I can handle the control room solo." I shrugged.

Brady ran a hand over his tight curls. "Harmon, go run."

Harmon's shoulders relaxed. The three moonkissed headed for the armor room, and the exit to the mist.

And then it dawned on me that Brady and I were alone. He set his mug in the sink and stood with his back to me. He was broad, and the shirt clung to him in all the right places, making it easy to see how built the guy was.

His shoulders rose and fell, and as he turned to face me, his hand went to the scar at his neck and rubbed it in a gesture I'd caught many times. I doubted he even realized he was doing it.

"Want some company in the control room?" he asked.

If I were clumsy and inept, I probably would have choked on my tongue because Brady was offering to hang out with me.

Brady, who spoke no more words than necessary, wanted to sit in a room with me ... voluntarily.

Keep it cool, Justice. "Sure."

HANGING WITH BRADY WAS SIMPLE. No need to speak. No need to make polite chitchat. There was just the beep of the monitors, a book, and two mugs of java.

Out of Lloyd's troop, he was now my second favorite hang-out buddy. Brady time was quiet time but with company. It was kinda perfect, and I felt my muscles unknotting and the tension leaving my body, and then my mind began to wander.

What kind of feyblood was he? He wasn't legacy, I knew that much. And he had a temper. Devon and Aidan were Opal pack, and Carlo was a Hartwood, but Brady kept his cards close to his chest. I studied him surreptitiously. His dark, bronzed skin, his harsh, bold features, and those dark eyes like a vast night sky. What could his heritage be?

"Stop thinking so hard." Brady's voice was a gruff rumble. "You got questions, then ask."

"That easy, huh?"

He turned the page of his book. "Yup."

"What kind of feyblood are you?"

"The angry kind."

O-kay. "And that would be?"

He closed his book and raised his dark eyes to mine. "I—" The beeping intensified, and Brady's gaze flew to the sector map. "Fuck."

One of the posts was blipping red.

I stood. "I'll get it."

He arched a brow. "Let me wake one of the guys to go with you."

"I can handle it by myself. Devon and Aidan are already out there. I won't be alone. I want to do this. Please."

"You sure?"

I smirked down at him. "Have you seen my maintenance record?"

Brady looked speculative but then nodded. "Okay. Radio up, and keep in touch."

Excitement bubbled up inside me. I was going to fix an AM post. I was going into the mist. And I was going alone.

THE MIST WAS FEY-MADE and housed goodness knows what kind of monsters, but a part of me craved being in it. It wrapped around me soothingly, blocking out the world for a little while.

Just me and a task.

High up on the post, the mist was thicker, but I'd worked the sim so many times my muscle memory for the task was excellent. One of three things could stop a post working. I ran through the requisite checks, and it took less than three minutes to get the post functioning again. The posts didn't have a battery pack because they siphoned energy directly from the air. The problem was usually the snap component, which acted as a convertor. We had plenty of replacements. I popped out the defective piece and slotted in a fresh one. The post hummed to life.

Done.

I was halfway down when I caught the shift of shadow in the mist to the far left of me. A figure. One of the guys maybe? No. It was too small ... and was that the flap of a cloak?

"Hey!" I scrambled down the post. "Wait!" I fumbled for my radio. "Brady, you there?"

"Yup."

"There's someone out here."

Silence. "Not the guys?"

"No."

"Get back to base. Now."

"But shouldn't I investigate?"

"No. Justice, get back to base. You hear me?"

Another shadow to my right. Not cloaked this time. Not the same figure—this one was bigger. Shit.

"Justice." The radio crackled and then died.

What? How the heck did that just happen? It was feytech, which meant it drew energy from the air.

A low moaning sound drifted through the mist ... a horn? The hairs on the back of my neck stood to attention. Time to get the fuck out of there.

I turned and ran. My inner compass clicked into action, and my feet steered me in the right direction. The sound of horns grew louder. They were behind me. They were in pursuit.

Who the fuck were *they*? I put on a burst of speed, ready to slip into blur mode, when the air behind me grew still, and then something landed on my back. The weight knocked me forward. My face slammed into the ground.

Something pressed to the back of my neck, a nose. Sniffing. Oh, fuck.

Softly whispered words were in my ear in a language I didn't understand. Then a hand gripped the back of my head, lifted it off the ground, and slammed it into the earth.

The world went black.

I came to with a jolt. My body was already in fight

mode, lashing out. Hands grabbed me, and the weight of a body pinned me down.

No! "Get off me." I bucked, trying to get free of the unrelenting weight.

"Stop. Please. Not hurt you. Save you."

The guttural words filtered through my panic. I stopped thrashing and intelligent violet eyes surrounded by gray hardened clay peered down at me. The face beneath the mask was lean and chiseled. Not what I expected of a fomorian.

"Not hurt you," he said again. "Save you."

Save me? "You knocked me out and took me."

His gaze clouded. "Save you." He frowned as if searching for a word. "Danger."

"I don't understand ..."

The distant sound of a horn drifted into the cave. Cave ... we were in the mouth of a cave. The catacombs? Was that where he'd taken me? I could get back from here. I knew the way home.

But then his grip on me tightened. He yanked on my arm, pinning me while pressing it to the ground.

"No. What are you doing."

"Save you," he said again. "Please."

There was something in his eyes, a desperation, a kindness that sucked the fight out of me.

I nodded.

He lifted my sleeve and pulled a slender dagger from a sheath at his thigh. His naked thigh covered in clay.

My brain made connections even as the knife registered. A naked fomorian with a dagger was holding a knife to my skin. Icy fear trickled through my veins.

I shrank from him. "Wait, what are you—"

His fingers on my arm tightened. "Save you. Please."

The panic that should have accompanied this situation was absent, and my gut was calm. Serene.

I nodded.

He pressed the blade to my skin, and then there was a sharp sting, a burning heat. He'd cut me, but it was over so fast I barely felt it, and now there was a weird symbol on my arm. Like an S trapped in an oval shape.

He released me and sat back.

"What did you do?"

"Gave you the ability to understand me." His voice was warm and no longer sounded guttural. In fact, it was almost melodic.

My gaze snapped to his. "You can speak my language?"

"Not well enough, but now that you have the scribe's mark, you can understand me. You're in danger. If they find you, they'll kill you."

"Who."

"The fir bolg. They wish to bring down your poison posts and will kill any fomori-touched they come across."

Fomori-touched? He must mean the shadow marked. "And you? Why are you here? Why did you save me?"

He sighed, looking almost weary. "I search for salvation, the blood that will free us." He frowned. "But instead, fate led me to you. To save you. No woman has found her way into the poison lands before, not that it would matter to the fir bolg. They would take you for sport." His lip curled in disgust at the thought before his expression cleared. "Why would the fomori-touched allow a woman into the poison lands?" He canted his head as if pondering his own question.

He didn't realize I was a shadow cadet—one of the fomori-touched. I guess the fact I was wearing a uniform didn't matter. Probably best to keep it that way.

Ignoring his question, which had seemed more reflective anyway, I looked to the mouth of the cave. "I need to get back. They'll be searching for me."

"Fomori-touched will be looking for you?" There was a calculated look on his face then. One that sent chills up my spine.

I shuffled away from him. "Look, I appreciate you saving me from these fir bolg creatures, but I need to go now. Okay."

He opened his mouth to speak, but a hacking cough emerged instead. He said something I didn't understand, but it had the inflection of a curse word.

His hand went to his chest. "Out of time."

The mist was affecting him. "You better get out of here." I stood and backed away from him, and he looked torn. "You'll die if you don't."

He clenched his teeth and shook his head. "The fir bolg can last longer. If they catch you—" He broke into a cough again.

He was one of them, a fomorian, but he'd saved me. "Will you be all right?"

There was sadness in his eyes. "I—"

The sound of a horn drifted in through the mouth of the cave again.

His jaw hardened, and he pulled himself up. Fuck, he was tall. A giant. "Fomori do not harm women, but fir bolg revel in it. I will lead them away. When the sound of horns retreats, run."

And then *he* was the one running—out of the cave and into the mists. The sound of horns rose in the air louder, excited, and then they began to drift away.

They had him. They were chasing him.

Dammit. None of this made sense. He was supposed to be the bad guy. Wasn't he? I needed to get back to the barracks and warn the others. There had to be an explanation for all this.

The world had gone silent as I ducked out of the cave and into the mist. I ran south, toward the barracks, checking my compass and wishing to hell that I'd brought my axes with me.

Not far now. Probably a quarter of a mile out. It

looked like the fomorian had carried me almost half a mile.

A howl to my left was followed by boot falls behind me.

My chest tightened then relaxed as the boot owner's scent hit me.

Brady. I slowed my pace, relief expanding in my chest.

"Justice." Brady grabbed my arm and turned me to face him, his concerned gaze raking over me. "Fuck. Where are they?"

Two wolves appeared out of the mist. Dark and shaggy, their heads as high as my shoulder.

Devon and Aidan sniffed me and growled. They could smell the fomorian on me.

"Justice, where did they go?" Brady asked again.

Shit. "Um, north."

I pointed in the direction the fomorian and the fir bolg had run. Devon and Aidan bounded off before I could stop them.

I gripped Brady's arm. "It was a fomorian. He saved me from the others. He called them fir bolg."

Brady ran his gaze over me again. He gripped my chin gently and coaxed my head to the side to scan the spot where the fomorian had planted his hand.

"He hurt you?"

"No. Not really. I mean he knocked me out and took me to the cave outside the catacombs. But he was trying to hide me from these fir bolg creatures." I stared up at him. "He was feeling the effects of the mist by the time we split, but he said the others, these fir bolg, could withstand longer periods in the mist. He called the mist poison lands. How can that be? I thought we were warding off fomorians. No one mentioned anything else."

"Yeah," Brady said. "So did I." His attention dropped to my mouth, and he released me. "Let's get you back to base. I need to call this in."

TWENTY-FOUR

W e were gathered in the whiteboard room, butts parked on the plastic chairs. The atmosphere was a mixture of apprehension and excitement. It had been an hour since the incident. Brady had taken a statement and ushered me to change and shower. By the time I'd gotten out, Vince was back with Hyde in tow.

The troop had been summoned, and here we were.

Hyde stood by the whiteboard, arms crossed, face like thunder. "After the incident in the mist, we've been instructed to increase patrols in all sectors. I'll be taking the first years back to the Academy and sending the rest of the second years to Vince for allocation."

Vince nodded, his face grim. "The fomorians must have found a new way to withstand the mist."

"No." I shook my head. "I don't think that's the case. The one that ... engaged with me. He was struggling to breathe, and he was covered in the clay you guys told us about."

"We pulled some clay off your hair. It's the same," Brady said. "Carlo ran tests on the composition."

Carlo raised two fingers. "I did, and it is."

"What about the fir bolg? It's this other race the fomorian mentioned that confuses me. He said *they* were the ones trying to bring down the posts, and *he* was looking for ... salvation or something. He could have killed me, but he didn't."

Hyde looked thoughtful. "Henrich, the shadow master, has been passed your statement of what happened. They are looking into it."

"Super soldiers?" Lloyd said softly. "Maybe these fir whatever are some kind of super soldier trained to spend longer periods in the mist."

"It will still kill them," Vince said. "The damage doesn't vanish once they get out of the mist. Damage is permanent."

"I doubt they care," Hyde muttered. "If they can take down enough posts, then they win."

"Two more posts went down around the time they were sighted," Brady said. "Just before Justice called in." He ran a hand over his face. "Lloyd and Harmon fixed them."

He had his head down as if he was ashamed or something. Shit, he was probably kicking himself over his decision to let me go out alone. But it wasn't his fault. I needed him to know that.

I tried to catch his eye, but he kept his dark gaze averted.

"A raid this far in ..." Hyde rubbed a hand over his mouth.

I rubbed the mark on my inner arm absently. It had healed but scarred, so it looked like a brown ink tattoo.

"And he gave you that so he could communicate with you ..." Carlo said softly, his gaze on my arm. "Doesn't sound like the actions of an evil fomorian."

No, it didn't.

"Fucking hell," Vince snapped. "So, one fucker saved Justice's ass. He could be here for any reason. Salvation? What the fuck does that mean? Probably some Otherworld religious nut getting himself mixed up in fomorian affairs. The fact is that this was a raid. The fact is that two posts were taken out. The fucking fact is these fuckers have found a way to get to sector one without dying."

There was a rumble of agreement from the cadets.

Hyde's gaze was fixed on me, but not on my face, on the mark on my arm. "We need to stick to protocol," he said. "Right now, the first years need to get back to the Academy." He dropped his arms to his sides. "I'll be back later," he said to Vince before turning his attention on Harmon, Thomas, and me. "Grab your gear. We need to head back. Now."

MASTER HYDE DIDN'T SPEAK ALL the way back to the Academy. Tension rolled off him like a menacing fog. He got us to the stone steps leading up to the shadow wing and stopped.

"Do not speak to anyone else about what happened today," he said. "The last thing we need is panic. The shadow knights will deal with this threat, and I'll inform Brunner when I return."

None of this made sense to me, and being cut off from the action was unfair. "Shouldn't we be helping?"

"Right now, you'll just get in the way. You've still got a lot to learn about the mist and the creatures that inhabit it. Focus on the trial. If you pass those, you're one step closer to being exactly what we need."

There was no arguing with that. I'd gone out without my axes today, a rookie error.

Harmon and Thomas began to climb the steps, and I made to follow.

"One moment, Justice."

Harmon looked back, but Hyde lifted his chin. "Carry on, you two."

Thomas continued up, but Harmon lingered a moment longer before following his lover up the steps.

Hyde looked down at me. "Are you all right? I know you said he saved you, but Brady said you got knocked out?" His hand came up and hovered by my cheek for a split second before he dropped it.

His gaze was warm. Not a tutor concerned about a

student but something more. No. I wouldn't do this again. He'd made his feelings, or lack thereof, clear.

I remembered to breathe. "I'm fine. The bump's already healed. He wanted to save me, and he had to knock me out to do that."

Hyde's expression smoothed out. "Then he's the exception to the rule. Fomorians may want a lot of things, but our survival is not on their list."

"Hell, what do I know? I've been doing this for a couple of weeks, and you've been doing it for years. But what I do know is that he could have hurt me, and he didn't."

Hyde sighed. "I'm glad you're safe. You shouldn't have been out there alone in the first place." His mouth tightened.

Crap, what if Brady got into trouble for this? "It was an AM post repair. It doesn't take more than one person to do, and Devon and Aidan were on patrol too. I wanted to go alone."

He took a step closer, and suddenly, there wasn't enough air between us. His proximity forced me to lift my chin to look at him. His lips were so close that if I pushed up on my toes, I'd be able to taste them. His eyes were hooded and heavy with desire.

Desire?

There was no imagining that. And just like that, my blood was rushing around my body in a frenzy of contradictive emotions.

"There you go," he said. "Being rash." His voice

thickened. "Being a shadow knight is all about being part of a team, Indigo."

I loved it when he said my name. "I'm all about the team efforts."

The warmth of his gaze made my mouth tremble with need.

Do it. Kiss me.

Oh, God. Just do it.

This was agony.

His breath brushed my cheek in the softest of sighs, and then he took a measured step back.

I caught myself before I could take a step with him and bit the insides of my cheeks to stop myself cursing.

His hands were fists at his sides as he studied me for a long beat, and in that moment, it was impossible to read him.

"I won't be formally reprimanding Brady." His tone was distant and cool. "However, in the future, all excursions into the mist must be undertaken in pairs. No exceptions."

He'd turned it off, whatever he'd been feeling, because there was no doubt in my mind now that he was attracted to me too. He just didn't want to be. Needles of frustration stabbed at my chest. "Fine. Is that all?"

"That's all."

I was pissed, but the reason was pathetic, and that made me more pissed. I turned on my heel and took the steps two at a time, anything to get away from the man who made me want to rip his clothes off one minute and punch him the next.

THE LOUNGE WAS BUZZING when I entered. I caught sight of Harmon and Thomas by the windows.

Thomas saw me, and then both guys were weaving their way through the crowd toward me.

"Justice." Thomas broke free of the throng.

"What's going on?"

"A cadet was found unconscious in the library. They took her to the med bay. Rumor is that it's the same shit that happened to Lottie and that other guy."

That didn't make sense. "It's been two weeks. If it was a virus, surely more cadets would have been hit with it before now."

"Brunner's issued a lockdown," Harmon said. "Everyone stays in their dorms." He snorted derisively. "Makes sense. Faraday's a legacy family, after all. They're going to pull out all the stops."

Wait, what? "Did you just say Faraday?"

Thomas shot Harmon a dirty look before turning back to me. "Indie. The girl they found in the library was Minnie."

LOCKDOWN MY ARSE. I paced my room. There was no

way I was sitting here twiddling my thumbs while Minnie was alone, frightened, lost. Fuck it.

I had to get to her. I had to see her.

There was only one way.

I stared at a pocket of shadow hugging the wall at the corner of the room. Please, let this work.

I ran into the darkness.

Oomf!

"Whoa!"

Hands steadied me.

"Indigo?" Master Payne looked down at me. "How ..." He glanced about. "Where did you come from?"

Shit on a stick. I'd materialized in the foyer to the med bay, not the quarantine room like intended because, of course, that room was too brightly lit.

Master Payne was studying me with a frown.

"I came to check on Minnie. I just walked in." I jerked a thumb at the door. "Through the door."

He didn't seem too convinced, but then what other explanation could there be, right? I saw the cogs turning as his gaze flicked from me to the door behind him, as he attempted to calculate how I could possibly have appeared in front of him and came to the conclusion that he must be going crazy.

"Yes, well ..." He released me and patted my shoulder awkwardly. "She's taking it well. Conscious and alert, but she already has a visitor. Maybe you should come back later?" His frown deepened. "Wait a second. Aren't we on lockdown?"

"Are we?" I blinked up at him innocently. "I just got back from shadow cadet duty. I didn't hear about a lockdown." I walked toward the quarantine bay and peered in through the round window to see the back of Harper's blonde head. My chest tightened. "It seems that Harper didn't get the lockdown memo either."

"Miss Bourne arrived with Miss Faraday. She was here when the lockdown was announced."

Of course she fucking was. I opened my senses, reaching out to hear what they were saying, and yeah, I didn't give a shit that I was blatantly eavesdropping in front of a tutor.

"I'm your best friend here," Harper said gently. "We do everything together. Don't worry about anything. I'll take good care of you. It's what we do—look out for each other."

Minnie was nodding. "Okay. Yes. That sounds good. Thank you." She sounded lost and small.

Her gaze slipped over Harper's shoulder and met mine through the window. A slight frown marred her forehead.

Harper followed Minnie's gaze, and her smile dropped. She patted Minnie's hand and then strode over to the door. She slipped out and closed the door firmly behind her.

Minnie was watching, her jade eyes wide with interest.

"What are you doing here?" Harper whispered.

"I came to see my friend."

Harper shot Master Payne a quick smile before returning her gorgon glare back to my face. "Minnie needs calm and quiet and stability right now. Things you can't give her. Where have you been the past two weeks anyway?"

Her words stung. "I have a trial coming up. I have to train."

"Yeah, you do. You have to do shadow cadet stuff. You don't have time to be here for her, not like I do."

"Miss Bourne," Master Payne said. "I hardly think it's up to you to decide who Miss Faraday's friends should be."

Harper's gaze snapped to Payne's. "With all due respect, *sir*, right now I'm the only person qualified to make those decisions. I've known Minnie most of her life. We grew up together. If anyone can help her recall who she used to be, it's me." Her stare bore into mine. "Can you honestly say I'm wrong? Can you promise you can be here for her as much as she needs?"

A vise squeezed my lungs, taking my breath, because she was right. As much as I wanted to stab her in the eye with a blunt pencil, the bitch was right. I swallowed my rage, my impotence, and my sorrow.

"Take good care of her." The words were broken glass.

Harper's body relaxed, and the harsh lines on her face softened. "You know I will." She retreated into the room with Minnie.

"Are you all right?" Master Payne asked.

But my mind was going off on a tangent, working on a new problem, one that I could help with.

I couldn't be there for Minnie, but maybe there was a way to figure out what had happened to her. "Where did they find her?"

"Excuse me?"

"In the library? Where in the library was Minnie found?"

"They've done a sweep of the place. They didn't find any clues," Payne said.

I looked purposefully into his gray eyes. "Maybe they were looking in the wrong place."

"What do you mean?"

"I have a theory, but we need to get to the library. Now."

TWENTY-FIVE

I t was a hunch. A stupid hunch, but if I was right then we'd know some things for sure. If I was right, there could be clues that the administration had missed.

Payne accompanied me, and the gargoyles on duty in the corridors slinked by us, leaving us be. He was a tutor, and I was in his care, so not technically breaking the lockdown.

The library was empty except for the librarian, Madam Florina. She looked up from her book as we entered and then quickly shoved the paperback under some papers. Probably a dirty romance novel.

"Carter?" Her cheeks reddened. "What can I do for you?" Her gaze slid to me in my shadow cadet black and blue. "Oh, a student out during lockdown?"

"Miss Justice is with me, Irina. Can you show us where Miss Faraday was found?"

The librarian nodded enthusiastically. "Of course. Follow me."

She clipped ahead in her neat one-inch heels, down the right side of the library, and past the contemporary fiction section to come to a halt near a small desk pushed up against the wall.

"She was found here," Madam Florina said. "I leave the library open during daylight hours for the odd students who choose to burn the dawn rays. I came in at sundown to find Miss Faraday slumped in this chair. Her books were on the floor."

Books? "Just textbooks?"

"Yes."

"What about notes?"

"Excuse me?" Madam Florina flashed Master Payne a confused smile even though I'd been the one asking the questions.

Master Payne smiled and patted her arm. "If Miss Faraday was studying, she would have had pens and notebooks with her."

Madam Florina shook her head. "No, nothing like that was found."

My pulse kicked up, and I barreled off through the stacks to the back of the library, cutting left and then right.

"Miss Justice?" Payne and Florina followed.

There it was. Minnie's nook. A half-drunk blood bag sat beside a set of neatly arranged pens and a notepad with a paragraph of writing in Minnie's cursive script.

"She was here. She was studying here. Whatever got her must have done so when she went to get more books and then dumped her at the other desk." I scanned the area, looking under the table and up the walls until... bingo. There it was, a copper grill vent. And clinging to the grill was some neon yellow gunk. "Look!"

Master Payne studied the residue.

My mind raced. "Something entered here and then ..." I scanned the floor to find more drops of gunk. "It tracked her."

Master Payne crouched to look at the droplets. "Madam Florina, do you have a pen pot I can have, please?"

PAYNE STARED at the gunk through a microscope.

I was hovering, but damn it, we had evidence in a pot. "Do you know what it is?"

"It's organic," he said.

"Okay. But where did it come from?"

He sat up and tapped his fingers on the countertop. "I've never seen anything like it."

"Maybe I can be of assistance?" Madam Mariana entered, bringing the scent of jasmine with her. "I bumped into Florina, and she told me about your discovery."

Payne blinked across at her. "Aren't you meant to be at the fortress?"

She smiled. "I was picking up some texts to take with me." Her gaze dropped to the microscope. "May I?"

I moved back to give her space.

She leaned across Payne's lap to peer into the eyepiece. "Hmmm. Organic. Alive, replicating. Interesting. Maybe a parasite of some kind?"

"The thought did cross my mind." Payne smiled warmly at her.

Madam Mariana glanced my way. "Maybe you should escort Miss Justice back to her dorm, Carter. I'll have another look at this sample and make some notes. I'm sure if we put our heads together, we can figure this out." She dimpled at him.

He cleared his throat, and the tips of his ears blushed. "I'll drop in and see Brunner. Let her know what we found."

She tutted and waved a dismissive hand. "We have no idea what this is yet. Better to go to her with answers, don't you think?"

Payne conceded with a slant of his head. He stood and steered me toward the door with a hand at the small of my back.

"Let's get you back to the shadow wing."

I could have shadow phased, but with Payne by my

side, it wasn't really an option. So we took the long route.

"How is shadow cadet life treating you?" Payne asked as he strode, hands in pockets, beside me.

"Good. It's good." Not much more I could say without breaking oath.

A gargoyle slipped out of the shadows and glared at us with orange eyes.

"At ease." Payne flicked a wrist in its direction.

The stone monster melted into the darkness once again.

"They creep me out," Payne said.

I looked up at him in surprise. "Really?"

He chuckled. "Really. We used to have one growing up. A gift from the council. They're usually inactive during the day, but here at the Academy the weavers have adjusted and modified the goyles to remain active around the clock if need be."

"They're also usually smaller, right?"

"Only the ones employed in regular households," Payne said.

"How do you know my parents?" The question just popped out. "Sorry, I just noticed you seemed to know them when they ... In the office the other day."

His step faltered. "Oh. Um, socially. Your parents and I attended prep academy together. Then I came here and they ... They got married."

"So, you were friends?"

He was silent for a long beat and then, "Yes. You could say we were friends."

We rounded the corner that led to the shadow wing and its barred entrance.

Payne slowed his pace. "You look a lot like her, you know. Your mother."

His words were like a cold bucket of water. "Yeah? Well, that's where the resemblance ends."

His eyes were sad. "We can't choose our family, but you have a chance to make a new family here with your friends."

He was right. Already, I felt as if Lloyd's troop and Harmon and Thomas were my new family, and Hyde ... Well, I didn't even want to dwell on what I wanted him to be.

Payne meant well, though, and snapping at him was pointless. "Can you let me know what you find out about the gunk?"

He nodded. "Of course. But your trial is in two days. You need to focus on that."

Shit. With everything that had been going on, the upcoming trial had momentarily slipped my mind.

I buzzed to get into the shadow wing.

"Lockdown, Justice. What do you think that means?" Larkin sounded pissed.

"She was with me," Payne said into the intercom.

There was a long beat of silence. "Well, that makes sneaking out of the dorm okay then, doesn't it?" Larkin said sarcastically.

The door clicked.

I winced up at Payne. "Sorry, and thanks for covering for me."

"It was worth it." Payne smiled, his eyes wrinkling kindly at the corners.

We parted ways, but it was only when I was climbing the stairs to the foyer that it hit me. Madam Mariana had said she'd gone to the library to pick up some books. Then why had she been empty-handed?

TWENTY-SIX

L loyd and his troop still weren't back at the dorms the next evening. In fact, the place was silent and dead. All the second years were gone, and it was just us newbies.

Larkin gathered us in the lounge.

"Master Hyde has instructed you to rest up today. Hopefully, the trial will still take place tomorrow. We'll know for sure later. In the meantime, do whatever people your age do."

"You want us to just chill?" Thomas asked.

Chill ... a word that hadn't been in my vocabulary for weeks.

Larkin's lips stretched in a wicked smile. "Make the most of it. It's the only day off you're going to get for a long time."

He winked out, leaving us sitting around feeling redundant.

"I wonder what's going on in the mist," Thomas said.

"Sweeps," Larkin's disembodied voice said.

"Shit!"

"Fuck!"

Several cadets yelped.

"Every time." Larkin chuckled. "Every time."

Thomas leaned back in his seat and smiled at Harmon. "A whole day to ourselves." He wiggled his eyebrows playfully.

Harmon drained his coffee mug and stood. "I'm going to get changed, then go see Lottie." He clomped toward the corridor leading to the dorm, leaving Thomas staring after him.

Someone snickered.

Thomas tucked in his chin, blinking rapidly. Shit, was he trying not to cry? I reached out, intending to pat his arm, offer some comfort, but he stood quickly and hurried toward the foyer.

Thomas would never be my favorite person, but he'd grown on me the past few weeks. I'd seen a side to him that was vulnerable and compassionate. One he'd kept carefully hidden before we'd been marked. What Harmon was doing to him was plain mean.

As much as I hated getting into other people's business, tonight I'd have to make an exception.

Harmon's room was the third one on the left. The door was slightly ajar, and I could hear him moving around. I knocked.

"Come in."

I pushed open the door to find him shrugging on a white T-shirt. His powerful chest was speckled with hair that tapered down his abs and vanished into the waistband of his joggers, and his skin was tanned and silken-looking.

"Don't," he said.

Shit, had he caught me staring? "Don't what?"

"Do not lecture me." He sat on the edge of his bed and pulled on his sneakers. "I'll talk to Thomas when I'm ready."

"And in the meantime, you're making him miserable." I stepped into the room and pushed the door closed. "Do you want to be with him?"

He raked a hand through his dark wavy hair. "That's none of your fucking business."

"Maybe not, but I'm sick of seeing him get hurt every time you blank him." I crossed my arms. "You're still fucking him, right?"

His jaw clenched, and then he glared at me. "Who I fuck is none of your business. You don't see me questioning your early evening sessions with Master Hyde, do you?"

My ears grew warm. "There is nothing going on between me and Master Hyde. He offered to train me, and I accepted."

"Is that what you call writhing on the ground then?"

Ice flooded my veins. "You were spying on us?"

"I went for a run. I saw you. That did not look like training. I see the way he looks at you when he thinks no one is watching. Hunger." He walked over to me and peered down his nose at me. "He wants to fuck you, Justice, and I think you want to fuck him too, but hey, who you fuck or don't is none of my business."

He was trying to turn this on me, to avoid discussing what was going on between him and Thomas, and if he'd simply asked me to back off, I would have, but like hell would I back down now.

"Do you love him, Harmon? Do you love Thomas."

His jaw ticked. "Fuck you, Indie." He turned away.

"Then stop hurting him. Tell him how you feel. Ask for some space if you need it. But don't make him feel like shit by ignoring him."

He stood, hands on hips, head bowed. "Everything is so fucked up right now," he finally admitted. "I need to focus on Lottie and training. I don't have room in my head for anything more."

"Then tell him that. Tell him what you want."

"How can I tell him what I want when I don't even know what I want."

"You can't keep stringing him along. It's not fair. If you can't get your shit together, then cut him loose. Be honest. If it's meant to be, you'll find your way back to each other, but right now, all you're doing is making him feel like crap."

His shoulders sagged, and my heart went out to him. "You're a good guy, Harmon. A little *grrr* at times, and you can be an asshole when you want, but you're not vindictive." I rubbed the spot between his shoulder blades. "What's happened to Lottie is fucked up, and Minnie ... I know how you feel."

He turned to me. "Lottie was a part of me, and now that part is gone. I see her and speak to her, but she isn't there. The kid I raised is gone. Those experiences, those memories that made her the Lottie I loved are gone." His throat bobbed. "It's like trying to love a stranger." His voice cracked. "It's like I'm forcing her to learn to love me back." He squeezed his eyes shut and pinched the bridge of his nose to hold back tears. "I fucking hate it."

My body acted on forgotten instinct. I wrapped my arms around his waist and pressed my cheek to his chest in a hug of comfort. His muscles tensed, and I made to pull back, but he circled me with his arms, and then he was hugging me back.

I'd been hugged by Minnie on several occasions, but a hug from Harmon was like a blanket being wrapped around me. It was safe and secure. Heat gathered behind my nose and pricked at my eyes as the contact began to unlock all the turmoil inside me.

There was a sharp rap on the door, and then it was pushed open. "Harmon, I—" Thomas's mouth fell open, and his eyes widened in shock.

Oh, shit. This looked bad. I made to pull away from Harmon, but his grip was firm.

Thomas turned on his heel and stormed off.

Harmon sighed and relaxed his hold on me. "I'll speak to him." He released me, almost reluctantly, and walked to the door. "Thank you."

This was what happened when I tried to fix shit. I just made it worse.

Urgh.

I left the cadet dorms and headed to the masters' quarters. A shower and fresh clothes were in order, and then I'd check in on Master Payne and the neon goop.

TWENTY-SEVEN

"You fool. You idiot." Larkin's voice drifted down the corridor. "You should know better. Let them do the work. You need to steer clear. It was a blessing."

"A blessing?" Hyde snarled. "You think this is a fucking blessing."

"Better than what could have happened. Playing with fire means you will get burned."

"Fuck you, Larkin."

"You wish."

They both fell into silence. Shit. Did they know I was there? Wait, why was I hovering at the end of the corridor? I lived here.

"Eavesdropping." Larkin materialized in front of me.

I pushed past him. "Going to my room."

I passed Hyde's door. It was open. He sat on the edge of the bed, and there was blood. Lots of blood.

"What happened." I rushed in and fell to my knees in front of him. His arm was covered in blood.

"I'm fine. Just the wrong place at the wrong time."

"You're no longer a shadow knight," Larkin said from the doorway. "Remember that." He vanished.

There was a bowl of water on the ground and several clean washcloths. Had Larkin been about to clean up the wound? I dipped a towel in the water, wrung it out, and began to wipe at Hyde's bicep. Three neat lacerations appeared beneath the blood. But they were already clotting up.

I winced as I cleaned, but Hyde didn't even flinch.

I peered up at him. "What did this?"

"A fomorian. We caught up to the raiding party where sectors two and three meet. They attacked."

"The fomorian said those raiders were fir bolg."

He snorted. "They looked fomorian to me."

"But surely they would have been gone by now. They can't stay in the mist that long."

"Henrich, the shadow master, believes this was another wave. A new raiding party."

"And you weren't supposed to be there?"

"I'm a tutor, not a knight." His smile was self-deprecating. "I teach others how to fight, but I'm no longer considered fit to serve."

"Firstly, I think that's bullshit. You have a bionic leg. That makes you even more kick-ass, in my opinion."

He arched a brow. "Really? You think my bionic leg

is kick-ass?" A smile hovered on his lips, and amusement sparked in his eyes.

My heart did a little skip and a jump because damn, he was fucking beautiful.

"Yeah ... Yeah, I do. I think ..." Don't say it. Just don't ... "I think everything about you is amazing. I think ..." I licked my lips. "I think you're beautiful."

Oh, shit, it was out there. Again. My heart was thudding so hard in my chest, I thought it would burst out of my ribcage. Blood rushed in my ears, like the call of the sea.

The smile on his lips wilted, and a storm churned in his eyes. "You shouldn't think those things, Indigo. You shouldn't say them. I thought I made that clear."

"Yeah, you did. But then you reach for me, or you look at me, and I can see you want me too." A fist squeezed my heart. "I get you don't want to feel ... whatever it is you feel for me. I know I shouldn't. But heck, I do a lot of shit I shouldn't do."

"And you're better than that," he said. "Better than me, better than most of the cadets out there." His hand was on my shoulder and then sliding up to cup the back of my neck. Heat radiated out over my skin where his palm and fingers made contact. He leaned in and pressed his forehead to mine. "Being a shadow knight is your calling, and you mustn't let anything come between you and your destiny."

Larkin's words came back to me now. "What did Larkin mean? What did he mean by *it was a blessing*?"

His fingers flexed on the back of my neck, and then he withdrew from me, sitting back to look at me with a hooded gaze. "That was a private conversation." His tone was suddenly glacial. He snatched the towel from my hand. "Thank you for your help, but I've got this."

What? That was it?

He stood and walked over to the sink and continued to clean his arm. "You can leave now, Justice. Go rest. The shadow knights have cleared the mist of raiders so the trial will be going ahead as planned." He met my gaze in the mirror, his expression unreadable. "Try not to die."

OKAY, so I'd promised to steer clear of Minnie, but tomorrow was the trial. It was life and death. And just in case I didn't make it ... I needed to say goodbye. Which was stupid because she no longer knew me, but still.

She opened her door with a polite smile. Same red bob. Same jade eyes, except there was no excitement to see me. No recognition.

"Can I help you?" she asked.

"I heard what happened to you. I just wanted to pop over and say how sorry I was and just ... basically, say hi."

"Did I know you?"

"We used to be roommates before I—"

"Oh, I heard about you. The female shadow cadet." She studied me carefully. "Harper didn't tell me you were my roommate."

Of course she didn't. "It may have slipped her mind." I bit the words out.

"Oh, gosh, yes. She's been inundated trying to fill me in on things. I don't know how I would have coped without her these past few days." There was real warmth in her tone. She canted her head. "Were we friends? I mean, did we hang out?"

This was my chance to tell her the truth, to tell her how she'd saved me, and how close we'd been. This was my chance, but I was leaving in a few hours. I was going to be walking into the catacombs in the mist and allowing myself to be sealed in, and I might not come back. Even if I did survive, my life belonged to the shadow knights.

And that felt right.

Minnie was a warm past. A beautiful memory.

She was looking at me expectantly. "Were we friends?"

"Not really." I shrugged. "I mean you were kind and invited me to stuff, but I wasn't really into it. Still, I wanted to say thank you. For being kind to me." On impulse, I leaned in and hugged her.

She stiffened and then slowly, achingly, she hugged me back. Fuck, I was going to bawl.

I pulled away quickly. "Yeah. See you around."

Walking away from Minnie, I allowed the grief to

wash over me. I allowed the single tear to fall and then dashed it away.

I rounded the corner, and the orange-eyed gargoyle that Payne had dismissed the other day blocked my path.

I glared at it. "We're not in lockdown anymore."

He shoved a piece of paper at me and then walked into the shadows and vanished. I studied the spot he'd disappeared. Was he still there or had he shadow phased like I could? That was a question for another day. I unfolded the paper.

MEET ME IN THE LAB, I FOUND SOMETHING. NOT A VIRUS. MASTER PAYNE.

My pulse kicked up. It wasn't a virus that had taken Minnie from me. Just as I'd suspected, there was something or someone out there that had targeted students, and Master Payne had answers.

I made it to the med bay in less than five minutes. The med bay foyer was shrouded in darkness, and the quarantine room was inky black and locked tight. The lab too was pitch black. I flipped a switch and lit it up. The microscope was still set up, but the pot of gunk was gone. There was no sign of Master Payne.

I took a step forward, and my boot tip contacted something. I crouched to examine the object. Green and bright and attached to a broken chain. It was an amulet. The same amulet Madam Mariana wore.

I plucked it off the ground just as the door behind me opened with a snick.

Madam Mariana stood in the doorway. Her gaze went from the amulet dangling in my hand to the microscope. Her face drained of color, and my scalp prickled in foreboding.

I gripped the amulet tighter. "Where's Master Payne?"

Her smile was forced. "Oh, he left early for the end-of-term vacation, I believe."

Why was she lying? "He sent me a note to meet him here. He said he had answers about the evidence we found."

She waved a hand. "Oh, that. We studied that residue. It was nothing. Just a secretion from a harmless fungus that grows in the vents. It thrives on humid temperatures."

"Wait, what? This place is fucking freezing. There is no humidity."

She looked over her shoulder, and when she turned back to face me, there was a deep weariness etched onto her face.

She gnawed on her bottom lip. "Dammit, child." She raised a hand, and green power jettisoned toward me.

Unconsciousness claimed me.

TWENTY-EIGHT

"Indigo? Indigo, wake up."

My eyes snapped open to Payne leaning over me. His blond hair had flopped onto his forehead, and two lines of concern sat between his brows.

The lab, the amulet. Madam Mariana. "Shit." I sat up quick, and my head spun.

"Easy." Payne steadied me. "The residue of Mariana's enchantment will take a moment to wear off completely."

I scanned the room through the bars of the cell we were in. The shelves and counters housed strange-shaped glass vessels with tubing running between them. A long counter with stuff on it. A lab. Alchemy? There was a counter with feytech armor balled up on it--feytech skin to be precise. The ceiling was rock face, the ground rough stone.

"Where are we?"

"Mariana's secret lab," Payne said. "It sounds like a bad joke, but I doubt whatever she has planned for us is funny."

"You found something, and she's involved?"

He nodded, his expression grim. "When we were examining the residue, she was dismissive. She kept saying it was nothing, but there was something too defensive about it all, so I did some more research. Florina showed me to the books on endangered supernaturals, and there was a book missing. She checked the catalog, and the missing book was on the history of morphs."

"Morphs? As in the creatures that can mimic organic matter?"

"Yes."

I was confused. "What has a morph got to do with anything?"

"I'm not sure," Payne said. But Florina helped me find another text with a page on morphs, and it mentioned a bright yellow secretion that morphs leave behind after they've adopted a form."

"What are you saying? That Minnie is dead? That the Minnie at the Academy is a morph?"

"No." Payne shook his head. "We did her bloodwork. She is definitely a nightblood."

"Then what?"

"I'm not sure. All I know is that there was a morph in that library and that it somehow took Minnie's memories."

"Leaving her intact ... but that isn't how morphs work, is it?"

"Not from what we understand about them, no."

"So, then ... we could be wrong?"

"Yes."

The door to the room opened, and a figure staggered in carrying something. No, not something, someone. Madam Mariana to be precise. She hung limp and lifeless in Redmond's arms. He laid her carefully on one of the countertops then stroked her hair back from her face.

Payne gripped the bars. "Redmond, what the hell is this?"

The Trial Master turned to us as if seeing us for the first time. "Oh, yes. You two." He looked down at Mariana. "Cora wanted to wipe your memories and let you go. But it isn't that simple anymore." He tugged at his hair. "Everything is messed up."

"Redmond." Payne's voice was calm and soothing. "Talk to me, man. Maybe we can work this out together."

Redmond shook his head vehemently. "There is no other way out. I must get rid of it all. I can't leave any evidence." He stroked Madam Mariana's cheek. "At least she won't feel a thing. It's one of her strongest concoctions. She just never expected me to use it on her."

"What is this place?" Payne asked.

"My lab." He looked to Mariana again. "Our lab.

This was our project, our way out of this fucking place, and now ..." His voice cracked. "Now, I'll have to do it alone."

"Do what alone?" Payne prodded. "Redmond, come on."

Redmond fixed his eyes on Payne. "Just six more years, that's all I have left before I can leave, before they give me what's owed to me. I've worked too hard to let anything come between me and my freedom." He looked down on Madam Mariana. "Not even you, my love."

My love ... So, Redmond and Mariana were a thing, and not Payne and Mariana. Was it those two I'd overheard in the lab the other day?

"Redmond." There was a snap to Payne's voice. "What do you know about the morphs?"

Redmond smiled weakly. "Everything. They were my ticket out of here. Did you know that morphs reproduce asexually when in their natural form? No? Not many people do. They breed once a year. All it took was one to breed an army of hounds, but I didn't think far enough ahead. I should have kept a couple of morphs aside in their natural forms, as backup, just in case my breeder died. But I was rushing. Wanting to get the trial ready last year. I had Mariana bind all the offspring into hound form. I should have asked her to leave a couple in their natural form," he chided himself.

"Wait," Payne said. "Are you saying you created hounds out of morphs?"

"Have you any idea how dangerous it is to catch a fomorian hound? I want to live to reap the rewards of this fucking position, and the damned knights at the fortress are adamant that we use feral hounds in the trials. Otherwise, I would have just taken some of our stabled ones and bred them, but the fucking stable hands keep track of everything. They've even named the hounds, and every knight is allocated one, so if any went missing, they'd notice. The bullshit they feed the cadets about the catacombs being a breeding ground is only half right. Like hell they'd allow it to grow out of control. They expect fresh hounds each year and slaughter the ones left alive after the trials."

"Archer always made it look so easy. Replacing the slaughtered hounds in a matter of days with fresh feral until he had his little ... *accident*." He cleared his throat.

Why had he said it that way? With that inflection ... Wait a minute. "Did you have something to do with it? Did you have something to do with the accident?"

He leaned back against the counter. "I needed that position. It should have gone to me, not a cadet just out of training."

"What did you do?" Payne's tone was hard.

He shrugged. "Mariana enraged the hound, which interfered with Archer's little hound whisperer trick."

I felt sick. "And then you played the hero and got him back to the barracks."

"Look, I didn't mean for him to lose a whole leg. Maybe a hand or just be badly injured. Long enough for me to step in and prove myself." He winced. "But it worked out more permanently than that, and I can't say I'm sorry. Mariana and I used the hounds Archer had already caught as templates to create our army. No one noticed. The trials since have gone smoothly, and the morphs have taken well to their new roles, even killed a couple of cadets. It was perfect."

Oh, God. He was crazy.

"Then what went wrong?" Payne asked.

How could he be so calm, so reasonable when talking to this madman?

Redmond scratched at his head. "The morphs in hound form started to lose it. Not a bad thing if they were going to be taking part in the trial, but then they started shifting in and out of hound form." He sighed. "The binding was losing its grip. Mariana ran some tests and realized the issue was with the breeder morph. The binding had somehow linked it to its offspring, and it was hungry. You see, morphs feed off the memories of the dead creature whose form they take, but these morphs hadn't been given that option. We'd manipulated them into existence and bound them using weaver magic, and they were slowly unraveling, so we had to get them memories."

"You brought the breeder onto Academy grounds," Payne said. "You let it feed."

"Yes, but we didn't kill anyone. Mariana put the

student into a deep death like slumber, which allowed the morph to feed on the memories, and because the breeder was bound in its natural form, it couldn't take on the student's form."

"You used the vents to get the breeder into the Academy?" Payne asked.

"It was the easiest way."

Anger bubbled up my throat. "The easiest way? You think any of this has been easy on anyone? You fucking wanker, you took their lives from them. You took my best friend away from me!" I rattled the bars, wanting nothing more than to grab him by the throat and squeeze.

His lip curled. "You have no idea what it's like. You're a child."

"Fix it. You have to fix it. Give them back their memories."

He looked at me blankly. "There is no fix. It's done. And that's why I must follow through, or they'd have lost their memories for nothing." He smiled, as if that was explanation enough, as if his words should reassure me.

The urge to break his face burned down my arm and coalesced in my fist.

Payne placed a hand on my shoulder. "Indigo, please ..."

His soothing tone took the edge off my anger, reminding me of the precarious position we were in. I took a deep breath and stood down.

"What are you going to do, Redmond?" Payne asked carefully. "Talk to me. Maybe I can help."

But Redmond had that stupid dazed expression on his face again, as if he was fucking high, and who knows, maybe he was. "I couldn't have done any of this without Mariana's weaver power. We were going to have a wonderful life, but she's lost her resolve. The breeder died a week ago, and the plan is unraveling. The morphs will soon break out of the bindings. There is no option but to get rid of them and start afresh. With the catacombs gone, I can offer the knights a fresh trial, one that doesn't involve my having to catch feral hounds." He stroked Mariana's cheek. "But you're not a killer, are you, my love? I can't blame you for that. But I can't let you warn Archer either."

Wait a second. "What do you mean with the catacombs gone?"

He blinked slowly at me. "Oh, it's all set up. I planted the explosives an hour ago. I'm going to cause a cave-in."

TWENTY-NINE

A cave-in. He was going to blow up the catacombs?

Oh, crap.

How long had I been unconscious? "What time is it?"

Redmond headed to the door. "It's time I left. The cadets will be here in a moment, and I need to open the doors and then seal them in." He had the grace to look guilty. "Seal you all in before the bombs go off."

Seal us all in. That meant ... We were in the catacombs. The lab was in the fucking catacombs.

"Wait, Redmond," Payne said. "You don't have to do this. I'll help you get rid of the morphs. We can keep this between us. If you do this, you'll be killing innocent students."

"That's what Mariana said." He took a step back into the room, his expression earnest, as if desperate for us to understand why he was about to murder us. "But don't you see, this is the only way to clear up this mess. A tragedy like this will make the knights rethink their trials. How many cadets have died in this trial in the past? Too many. It's pointless death. This way, I kill two birds with one stone. I cover up the mess I've made, and I save future cadets from this pathetic ritual. In a few minutes, the cadets will be sealed inside, and two hours later, the bombs will go off. They will be martyrs to a greater cause."

"Is that what's going to help you sleep at night?" I felt sick. "You're a murderer, plain and simple. A greedy fucking murderer."

Redmond ignored me and opened the door.

"Redmond, stop. Please, reconsider," Payne implored.

"I'm sorry, I wish it hadn't come to this." Redmond's mouth turned down. "But I can't risk losing my position."

The door closed behind him with a firm click.

Payne grabbed the bars and tugged. He began to examine the cell, looking for weaknesses. Looking for a way out. My attention was drawn to the pocket of shadow in the corner of our prison.

Fucking hell. I'd had an out all along. I could have leapt out and smashed Redmond's smug face in.

I made a sound of exasperation, which drew Master Payne's attention.

"Don't worry, Indigo. We will find a way out of this." His mouth said one thing and his eyes another.

He was right, we could get out of here, but it would mean exposing my secret to Master Payne.

There was no choice.

If I didn't act now, cadets would die. "I know we will because I can get out of here, but you have to promise me you'll keep what you see to yourself."

He frowned. "If you can get out of this cell, then do it."

"Promise me."

He made a sound of exasperation. "I promise."

I took a deep breath, visualized the other side of the room, and then ran into the shadows.

I stepped out facing Master Payne, still locked in the cell. His mouth was hanging open.

"I call it shadow phasing." I searched for a key to the cell.

There, by the weird test tube thing. I grabbed the key and raced to the cell to let Master Payne out.

"We have to get to the entrance to warn the others," Master Payne said. He looked at Mariana's sleeping form. "The catacombs are a maze. You'll need to go without us. Phase out to the entrance. Can you do that?"

"What time is it?"

Payne looked at his watch. "Ten after nine."

"It's too late. The cadets are already in here. There is no way out."

"This place is used for trials. The seal is on a timer, so once it's shut, it won't open until the trial is up. But there must be another way in. A back door. But only someone who ran a trial would know."

My pulse leapt. "Hyde."

"Yes." His eyes lit up. "You need to get to Hyde. Tell him what's happened. He might have a map. We have two hours before the bombs go off. You can do this, Indigo."

"I don't want to leave you here. Maybe I can take you with me?" Although I hadn't thought about carrying a passenger, what harm was there in trying.

"No." Payne shook his head. "This ability is new, right? Untested?"

"Well, I know I can get from one pocket of shadow to another if I focus on a place or person. I end up as close to them as the shadows allow."

"But have you carried anyone?"

"Not yet, but ..."

"Then we can't risk it." His tone was firm. "Every ability comes with a consequence. It's why weavers have the amulets to recharge when they use their weaver power. Whatever this ability is, it will have a cost. Usually a cost to your energy levels. Carrying someone could drain you and make it impossible for you to get back in with a map." He cupped my shoulders. "You have no choice. You need to leave me here. You're our only hope."

He was right.

As much as I hated to leave him there, there was no other choice.

I grabbed the feytech skin off the counter. "You'll need to turn around while I get changed."

He obliged. "Why?"

I quickly shrugged out of my slacks and shirt and pulled on the feytech. "The mist isn't kind on manmade materials. Makes me wonder how Marianna got us here. She couldn't have gone through the mist without armor."

"Weaver enchantment?"

"Possibly. I'm done."

He turned to face me and nodded curtly. "You can do this, Indigo."

I blew out a breath and latched on to a pocket of shadow. "I'll be back."

Picturing Hyde in my mind, I ran into darkness.

COOL AIR and mist surrounded me. I was outside, but where was Hyde?

An arm pressed to my throat, and I was hauled back against a breastplate. Citrus aroma tickled my senses.

"Hyde. Shit, it's me."

He released me abruptly. "What the fuck are you playing at, Justice? You missed the trial. Do you know what that means?" He looked me over. "Where the fuck is your armor?"

"I didn't miss it, I was kidnapped." I filled him in using the cliff notes version, watching the confusion melt into comprehension across his face. "And Master Payne and Madam Mariana and all the cadets are going to die if we don't get them out." I scanned his face, watching the cogs turning. "Is there a back door to this place?"

He nodded. "Yes."

"Can you draw me a map?"

"No." He tapped his head with an index finger. "The map is up here. I need to be inside the catacombs to use it."

Shit. The door was sealed. There was no way for him to get in ... unless ... unless I took him with me. Master Payne had said there could be a cost to carrying someone. It could leave us stranded inside ...

But that wouldn't matter if we had a way out. "Maybe I can get you inside."

"What?"

"I mean this shadow phasing thing ... Maybe I can take you with me?" I threw up my hands. "Look, it's worth a try, isn't it?"

He nodded. "Fine, let's give it a shot. But if it doesn't work, if you find yourself alone in there, you get your arse back out here stat, you understand me?"

I nodded mutely.

"How long till the bombs go off?" he asked.

"Two hours after the start of the trial."

He glanced at his watch. "We have an hour and a half. We can do this."

I scanned the mist for shadows and settled on the mouth of the cave that was dripping with darkness. Harmon ... I needed to visualize Harmon because if I knew that guy, he'd be leading the troops.

I held out my hand. "Are you ready?"

Hyde slipped his hand into mine, palm to palm, his long fingers wrapping around mine. My heart sped up.

"Let's do this."

We ran into the shadows together.

THIRTY

R ock surrounded us, and the scent of death and decay pressed in on me. We were in a narrow tunnel with a ceiling low enough to jump up and touch, or for Hyde to just reach up and press his palm to. Soft green light illuminated the tunnel. It was coming from a glowing mossy plant that covered the rock in patches.

"Urgh." Hyde covered his nose and mouth with his free hand.

Yeah, it was an overpowering smell, and my gag reflex sprang into action. I adjusted to breathing through my mouth, which was just as gross because it meant I was tasting the air. I took a step, and the world swayed as dizziness assaulted me. Okay ... this had to be the effect of carrying someone. Not so bad. I could deal with this. Just one moment.

"Justice, you okay?" Hyde asked.

I smiled. "Fine. Just a little dizzy."

He frowned. "The phasing ... fuck, it's taking a toll, isn't it?"

But the dizziness had dissipated. "I'm fine. Harmon should be close by. We need to get to him."

Shouts and bellows drifted down the tunnel toward us.

To demonstrate how fine I was, I broke into a run, taking Hyde with me. It was only when we skidded around the corner and came face to face with a bunch of cadets fending off three hounds that I realized we were still holding hands. I released him abruptly.

He drew a dagger from his belt and handed it to me. "I know we haven't trained much with daggers but—"

"I can handle it."

We jumped into the fray.

Harmon and Thomas were back to back, hunting daggers and swords flashing as they fended off the beasts. One cadet was on the ground, slumped against the wall, clutching his abdomen, while another applied pressure to a bubbling wound. Mal ... Mal was down, face pale, eyes too dark in his head. His body shook as it went into shock.

Helping him would have to wait till we'd dealt with the hounds. Not real hounds but just as dangerous. Their eyes were bright red, and feral rage motivated their every move. Harmon caught sight of me, and almost got snared by the snap of powerful jaws.

"Justice!" he cried out. "Get back."

Yeah, not happening. I stabbed the hound in the neck, slicing into its vertebrae. It went down, oozing yellow gunk.

"What the hell?" Thomas cried out.

I shook off the gunk on my hand. "They're not hounds, they're morphs. I'll explain later. We need to get out of here."

Behind us, Hyde had already dispatched the other two hounds.

He stood, magnificent, chest heaving as he scanned the room. "We're missing three cadets?"

"They ran that way when the hounds attacked." Thomas's lips curled in disgust. "Cowards."

"He's lost too much blood," the cadet administering to Mal said.

It was Gimble, the sandy-haired dude with the large Adam's apple.

Mal looked up at us, his breath coming in shallow pants. "Don't ... don't want to die."

Fuck.

"He needs blood." Harmon rolled up his sleeve, but Gimble beat him to it, shoving his arm into Mal's mouth.

"Fey blood is more potent," he said by way of explanation. "I don't know what ... I didn't think ... I should have ..."

"Logic can fly out of your mind in the heat of combat," Hyde said kindly.

"See that, Mal?" Thomas sneered. "A bastardized fey is fucking saving your ass."

But Mal was too busy slurping, and Gimble's eyes began to flutter closed. The fucker was draining him.

"Enough!" I kicked Mal in the head, hard enough to dislodge his fangs from Gimble's arm.

The feyblood fell back with a moan.

"Shit." Harmon swept him up and over his shoulder.

Mal shuddered as he healed, wounds knitting, and the scent of Gimble's blood had saliva pooling in my mouth. I swallowed and stepped away from the semi-conscious feyblood.

Mal used the wall to stand, his dark, angry eyes confused and clouded for once. He'd almost died, and that shit could change a person. Let's hope it gave him a personality overhaul.

"We need to move," Hyde said. "Come on." He led the way away from the dead hounds bleeding yellow gunk, and down the corridor the other cadets had taken. "They can't have gone far. From what I recall, the hounds like to make their dens this way. Plenty of nooks to curl up in. Let's hope they haven't gone too deep." A scream echoed off the walls. "Stay here," Hyde ordered, and then he ran toward the screams.

Like hell was I letting him get his arse killed. He was our only way out of here. "Stay here," I said to Harmon, mimicking Hyde's tone. "Trust me. We're here to get you all out. This place is rigged and about to blow."

"What the—" Harmon made a grab for my arm, but I was already running after Hyde.

The tunnels narrowed claustrophobically, interconnecting and shooting off from each other. It was a warren, a dark, dank warren, and if not for the grunts and growls, I would probably have gotten hopelessly lost.

I skidded into a wide chamber to find a cadet cowering in the corner and two on the ground. From the looks of the pulpy mess of their torsos, they were dead.

Hyde fought off two hounds larger than the ones we'd come across in the previous chamber. These were full grown ones. Morphs too if the yellow lacerations on their hides were anything to go by. This was why Redmond hadn't wanted Hyde to kill the hounds that had escaped into the forest. The yellow gunk would have been a dead giveaway.

"Get the cadet out of here," Hyde ordered.

"I'm not leaving you." I ducked and dove, and then my back was to Hyde's. "We get out together."

We defended and attacked, covering each other against the beasts, trying to get close enough to stab an artery—if morphs had arteries, that is. A claw scraped my arm, eliciting a yelp.

"Justice?"

"I'm fine." I slammed the hilt of my blade against

the beast's head and kicked out to give myself some breathing room, but the reprieve was momentary, only enough to take a breath. Then the hound was lunging again, red eyes wide and insane.

This was Redmond's fault.

These had been intelligent creatures once.

He'd done this, and it was time to end it. It was time to put these creatures out of their misery.

"I'm sorry. So sorry."

It took four punctures to find its main artery—right under its chin—and it went down instantly, convulsing as it bled out yellow goop.

I turned to help Hyde only to see him kick out with his bionic leg and send the hound flying into the wall. There was a crack, and then the hound slid to the ground, unmoving.

I sagged in relief. We'd done it. Oh, God.

Hyde turned on me, eyes blazing. "I told you to stay put. What the fuck were you thinking?" He shouted the words, anger twisting his beautiful features and making the scars stand out bloodless against his flushed face.

What was *I* thinking? *Seriously*? Rage rushed through me like an inferno, and then I was closing in on him, eyes burning with the heat of indignation.

"I was thinking that I couldn't bear for anything to happen to you! I was thinking if you die, we all die. I was thinking I needed to save your fucking ass."

We stood chest to chest, breath coming fast and

shallow, eyes locked, and then with a ragged groan, he wrapped his hand around my ponytail and yanked me toward him. His mouth slanted down over mine, hungry, crushing, desperate, as if I was the oxygen to his flame. Citrus and salt on my tongue, an aching bloom in my heart. Heat behind my eyes because this was it. This was the connection I'd been yearning for. He sucked on my tongue, and then pulled back, grazing my bottom lip with his teeth as he broke the kiss.

My insides were a molten lava of need, and my knees were rubber. His eyes churned with all the emotion he'd been holding back these past weeks, and in that moment, I was ready to drown in them. In that moment, I was just a woman falling in love.

"Fuck," he said softly, lids and lashes at half-mast. "Damn you, Justice." He released me reluctantly and puffed out his cheeks. He closed his eyes and shook his head slightly, his tongue flicking out to sweep across his bottom lip as if savoring me there. My core tightened. "We can't do this now," he said gruffly. "Let's get the cadets out of here."

Not now but later. We'd do this later? The giddy part of me, the part that had been locked in chains forever, perked up, but I slapped her down. Not the time or place.

We ran back through the tunnels, picked up the others, and followed Hyde through the network.

He moved with ease, like he knew this place, like

he belonged there. He stopped now and then to touch the wall or study a crack and then continued. My inner compass kept track of the direction. East, always east. I needed to know which way we were headed because I wouldn't be leaving with them. It was obvious Hyde hadn't thought that far yet, and I wasn't about to remind him, not until the last minute because there was no doubt in my mind that he'd try to stop me.

A soft rumble drifted down the corridor toward us and Hyde froze and raised a fist, signaling for us to stop.

He looked back at us. "Wait," he said softly, and then he crouched and continued forward.

The darkness swallowed him. Long seconds passed and then he reappeared. Was it my imagination or had his face drained of color?

He looked over his shoulder. "There's a nest up ahead. Sleeping hounds. But there's enough space to get past if we go single file."

Harmon had Gimble around the waist and was practically holding him up. The feyblood was still weak from feeding Mal. The others looked shell-shocked and ragged, and we'd been expected to survive down here for half a day? Fuck that. Redmond was insane but he'd had a point about this trial being dumb.

"I'll take Gimble," Mal said. "I can carry him."

The nightblood looked flushed and filled with

energy, not surprising since he'd supped on feyblood. The stuff was potent shit.

Harmon passed Gimble to Mal.

Hyde nodded. "Move carefully, keep silent. We got this."

"And if they wake up?" Thomas asked.

Hyde's nostrils flared slightly. "Then we fight."

But there were only a handful of us left and one of us was injured. If it came down to fighting a nest of hounds we were fucked, and everyone knew it.

Deathly quiet it was, then.

Hyde led the way down the tunnel. It widened and then the hum and rumble grew louder. The green glow was dimmer here, but there was enough light to see the hulking sleeping shadows of several hounds lying on the ground. Nooks and ledges dotted the walls and hounds were tucked into those or sprawled across them. So many hounds. Too many hounds.

We were outnumbered two to one.

Our shallow breaths mingled with the rumble of the sleeping hounds. Just a little way to go. The exit loomed ahead, dark and inviting. Don't look back, just keep moving. How could Hyde be so nimble with his bionic leg.

He moved fluidly, he moved silently. I mimicked him, placing my feet where he placed his, blocking out the fact we were surrounded by monsters.

And then we were through the arch. Hyde pulled me aside and pressed me to the wall. His eyes gleamed in the darkness and his mouth parted on a soft exhale. I wanted to swallow it, to press myself to him and revel in the heat of his body and the beat of his heart.

He blinked slowly and a silent communication passed between us, one that didn't need words. One that said, we made it, we're okay. One that said, later.

The others began to join us in the tunnel beyond the nest and Hyde released me and ushered everyone forward.

I counted heads as they came through. Almost there.

A sharp male yelp cut through the hum of sleep.

My body froze, tensing up in horror. Hyde's gaze flew to mine and then back to the arch leading to the nest.

Silence.

Actual silence. No rumble. No sleep.

"Oh fuck!" Hyde rushed forward, drawing his sword and pushing the cadets aside.

I was right behind him.

Someone screamed and then all hell broke loose.

THIRTY-ONE

No time to think, no time to plan. My body was in auto-fight. My dagger slicing, cutting, maiming. I defended and attacked, rolled and ducked. The world was a blur of instinct and the potent scent of blood. Cadet blood. My blood. But wounds would heal.

Keep going. Keep fighting.

I caught a glimpse of Hyde putting himself between Gimble and a hound by shoving the feyblood back toward the exit.

Thomas used one arm to support the feyblood and the other to beat back the hound that was intent on attacking them. I cut a swathe through the fray and buried my dagger in the hound's head.

Thomas's gaze met mine.

"Get him out." I turned just in time to fend off a fresh hound.

Shit, how many were there?

Harmon and Mal fought back to back. Hyde? Where was he?

There, in the center of things, surrounded as usual. It was like he attracted trouble. I rushed toward him, dagger at the ready. It sliced, snagged and drew yellow goop. Howls of pain, growls, and snarls cut the air, and then I was in the center and Hyde was cursing but there was a crazy grin on his face which swelled my heart. This felt right. It felt natural. We fell into sync, fighting as if it was a coordinated dance and it was as if we'd been doing this forever. As if it was meant to be. My limbs burned with euphoria as we brought down hound after hound until I was standing amidst a sea of bodies.

My body was vibrating with energy. I turned to Hyde to find his gaze on me, dark and hungry and dangerous. Heat bloomed at my core. Want and desire and the desperate need for him to break and take me now. Fuck what was this? What was this violent, ravenous need aching and throbbing between us? He took a shuddering breath and shook his head as if to clear it.

"We need to go. Now," he said. "The scent of death will no doubt draw more hounds."

With a final lingering look my way, he climbed over the dead hounds and strode toward the exit.

We were covered in goop, tired, and wary as we

navigated the tunnels. Hyde moved faster than before, forcing us to keep up or lose our way.

He finally came to a halt by a section of smooth rock. "Here," he said.

"What?" Harmon asked. "What are we looking at."

Hyde pressed his palm to the wall, and it shimmered to reveal a round hole. "Master Henrique put it in a few years ago," Hyde said. "Only the shadow knights and the trial master know of its existence. It leads out of the catacombs." Hyde ushered the first cadet into the hole. "Just keep climbing," he instructed. Thomas went next.

Harmon turned to me. "Now you."

Oh, crap, this was the moment. "I can't." I backed away.

"Justice!" both Harmon and Hyde snapped at the same time. Agitation was rife in their tones.

They exchanged surprised glances at the jinx moment.

There was no time to argue. No time to debate. "Get out." I turned away and focused on a spot of shadow. "I'll find you, but you need to be outside."

I closed my eyes and visualized the route we'd come, praying I could find it again.

"I'll be back." I turned away.

"Justice!" Hyde growled. "I know you want to save Payne, but there's no time. He wouldn't want you to risk your life for him." He grabbed my hand and pulled me toward the exit.

I tugged free of him. "I can phase there."

"Dammit, Justice, you have no idea where the lab is or how far it is from this exit."

I backed away from him. "I know the route. I'll find it. I can't leave him to die."

Something dark and desperate flashed across Hyde's face. "Promise me, if you get stuck for time, if you get lost, promise me you'll phase to me."

"I promise."

"What the fuck is going on?" Harmon asked.

Hyde drew me close, his expression intense, his eyes burning across my face as if committing it to memory. "Do not die."

There were words between us, so many words, but neither of us spoke them. Instead, I pulled out of his arms and dove into shadows.

PAYNE LOOKED up as I stepped into the lab, but my vision went dark for a moment, and my knees grew weak.

"Indigo." Payne grabbed me in time to stop me from falling. "What did you do?"

I brushed him off. "I carried Hyde into the catacombs. I'll be fine in a minute."

"You managed to carry someone?" Payne's eyes lit up.

"Later. Let's get you out of here first."

We turned to Madam Mariana to find her awake and sitting up.

"What ... What happened?" Her eyes widened when she realized where she was and who she was with. "Oh, no."

"Yes," Payne said. "Redmond betrayed you. Now if you want to live, you better come with us."

Mariana stood on shaky legs. "How long?"

I glanced at the clock. "Ten minutes." I pulled open the door. "Mariana, you got any mojo?"

She flexed her hands. "Yes."

"Good, because if we come across any morph hounds, then we'll need you to use it."

We stepped out of the lab and into a foyer. A set of steel doors greeted us. Mariana used her palm print to open the doors, and then we were spilling into the catacombs.

Which way? Shit.

I let my gut take point through the catacombs. East. I had to go east. Howls and growls drifted toward us, but we moved away from them, and suddenly, the tunnels began to look familiar. We were on the right track. My legs buckled, and Payne grabbed me around the waist, hauling me up.

I shook my head, willing my body to cooperate, and continued. "This is it. This is the way." I picked up the pace, ignoring the burn in my limbs. The price for phasing too often in a short period, for carrying another person. Once we were out of there, I'd rest.

The edges of my vision darkened. No. Not yet. Keep going, but we'd barely gone several feet when the thunder rumbled through the tunnel and the ground rocked.

"Oh, no," Payne said. "It's happening."

The tunnel shook, and chunks of rock rained down on us.

"It's too late," Mariana said.

"Go," Payne said to me. "You should have enough energy to phase out of here by yourself."

I'd promised Hyde. I'd promised, but how could I leave Payne and Mariana to die? Another quake rocked us, and the tunnel ahead collapsed. We were trapped.

Payne grabbed my shoulders and shook me. "You need to go. Now."

Shadows pooled behind him. This might not work, but I had to try.

Comprehension bloomed on Payne's face as he read my expression. "Indigo, it could kill you."

"Or it could save us all." I gripped his hand and made a grab for Madam Mariana's cuff.

Hyde, I'm coming.

I fell into the shadow patch, taking them with me.

Pain ripped through my head, tearing at my limbs, burning through my mind. My scream filled my head.

"Back up, give me room."

I knew that voice.

Mariana.

Alive.

Had we made it?

Where was I? Why couldn't I see.

Cool hands on my forehead. Soothing. Calm. The pain ebbed, and my vision slowly returned to mist and figures standing around me.

"She's okay," Mariana said.

"Get away from her," Hyde snapped, and then his face was hovering over me, his expression one of relief. "Dammit, Justice." He hauled me to my feet and then swung me up into his arms. "Are you ever going to stop being so fucking rash?"

I was woozy and shaking, but fuck, I was alive. I wrapped my arms around him. "It's gonna take work, Hyde. I hope you're up to the job."

And then I allowed exhaustion to claim me.

THIRTY-TWO

My body ached, but the fever that had gripped me was gone, leaving me sweaty but cool. How long had I slept? The room was dark, but someone had turned on my lamp.

Hyde had tucked me into bed. I remembered that much, even though my eyelids had been too heavy to keep open.

I lifted the covers to find myself fully dressed.

There was a knock at the door, and then Hyde entered the room carrying a blood bag and a napkin.

"Good, you're awake."

I sat up and groaned. "I feel like shit."

"The effects of carrying people while phasing." He sat by my hip and passed me the bag. "Drink."

My gums ached for real blood, blood from the vein, and for the first time since killing the human, panic didn't seize me. Instead, a deep sorrow permeated my soul, followed quickly by anger ... Anger at my father for doing this to me. For turning me into a murderer and leaving this stain on my soul.

"Drink," Hyde ordered.

I did as I was told. The blood was warm, perfect, and it was gone too soon. I paused for breath. "How long have I been out? What did I miss?"

"The evening and the day. We lost two cadets, and one was in the med bay. The catacombs are gone, and so is Redmond. Mariana has been taken into custody, and the whole Academy is buzzing with the news of the incident." He took a deep breath and sucked his bottom lip into his mouth. "You could have died today." His throat bobbed.

I put down the empty blood bag and licked my lips to compose myself. "Yeah, but we knew that going into the trial."

Hyde sighed. "No, I was never worried about you in the trial. You have the makings of a warrior. You would have survived."

His confidence in me gave me all the warm and fuzzies.

"But the cave-in," he continued. "When those bombs went off ..." He trailed off and looked away.

His hand curled into a fist on his lap.

"Hey." I covered his fist with my palm. "I'm all right." I inhaled him.

He closed his eyes. "We can't do this, Indigo."

"Do what?" My voice was a whisper because I

needed him to say it. To confirm what was hovering between us with words, not just action.

He swallowed and pinned me with that beautiful gaze. "You know what."

I had to touch him, and before I could, my fingers were at his temple, running along the scars that crossed his face, fingertips grazing his lips. His tongue peeked out to taste at the pads of my fingers, and my breath hitched.

He grabbed my wrist, pulling it away from his mouth. "Indigo." My name was a breath.

I leaned in, tilting my face to his so our lips were mere centimeters apart. "Archer."

His eyes darkened with dangerous hunger, and then he broke for me with a low growl. His hand came up to tangle in my hair, fingers cupping my scalp, and his lips claimed mine in open-mouthed carnal kisses that seared me. Tongue and teeth and wanton need bubbled between us, and then I was kissing air.

Hyde stood on the other side of the room with his back to me. "Fuck," he said softly.

"I wish."

"No." He shook his head. "This didn't happen. The kiss in the cave didn't happen."

But they had, and I could still taste him on my throbbing mouth. "Archer."

His shoulders rippled with tension. "Master Hyde." He turned to me, his mouth swollen from my kiss. "I'm your tutor, that's all I can be. That's all I want to be. Do you understand?"

The euphoria in my chest dissipated, and the arguments died on my lips because he didn't want this ... this thing between us. This unwanted attraction was tearing him apart.

He puffed out his cheeks. "This isn't why I came in here. I didn't come here to ..."

"I know that." Fuck, I couldn't look at him. Not without my heart shining out of my eyes.

This wasn't me. I wasn't a romantic. I didn't lose my heart. I fucked, fed, and moved on. How could this be happening to me? How could this hurt so much in such a short space of time?

Hyde cleared his throat. "Master Payne would like to work with you on your shadow phasing, to figure out how it works, and how you can utilize it without hurting yourself."

Back to business then. Fine. I could do that.

I nodded. "Okay." I crossed my arms. "Anything else?"

He looked pained but continued. "Mist duty continues, but Henrich, the shadow master, has decided that due to the small number of cadets in year one, and the increased raiding activity of the fomorians, you should all be fast-tracked and amalgamated into the second year."

"What?"

"You'll be starting classes at the fortress after the term break," he said.

My heart pumped faster at the news. The fortress ... We'd be getting to study there?

"Which also means I'll be handing over most of your training to Master Venrick," Hyde continued. "He's a veteran shadow knight, and a good friend of mine."

My heart sank and anger licked at my chest. I didn't bother to hide my disgruntlement. "So, you won't be training me anymore."

It was as if he was punishing me for this attraction that simmered between us. As if it was all my fault.

He closed his eyes and exhaled. "You don't need me, Indigo. You may be rash, and impulsive at times, but you saved a lot of lives today. I'm proud of you."

And just like that, the anger melted. Damn him. I stared at him, raking my gaze over his beautifully scarred face, heart squeezing painfully and throat pinching.

"Thank you."

The air between us crackled with tension and the magnetic pull that came from an inexorable attraction. An attraction I couldn't deny, and one he didn't want.

Hyde took a shuddering breath and deliberately moved farther away from me. "Get some rest, Justice. The term may be over, but shadow cadets don't get any time off. Mist duty starts tomorrow."

And then he was gone.

LLOYD'S TROOP, Harmon, Thomas, and I sat around the lounge drinking cocoa made by Lloyd. There was a shroud of reflective silence.

"She didn't know me," Lloyd said. "I went to see her, and she looked at me like I was a stranger."

Minnie.

I'd avoided that painful place. Avoided having to see the lack of recognition in her eyes.

"I know, man," Harmon said. "Trust me, I know what it's like."

"My parents are in consultation with the head weaver at headquarters," Lloyd said. "Maybe they can do something." He smiled sadly at Harmon. "I'll let you know what happens."

Harmon nodded slowly, then sipped his cocoa.

To have Minnie back ... Could that be a possibility? Her loss was a hole in my heart, the one right next to the crater Hyde had dug.

Urgh.

Brady entered the room, and my body went into alert mode. There was no denying the monolith had a commanding presence, which made me wonder why he was Lloyd's second and not the troop leader.

His attention went straight to me, lingering there before drifting over the guys. "Are you fucking kidding me? We have the night off, and you bitches are sitting here drinking cocoa?"

Carlo entered the room carrying a football. "I told you they were being old maids, didn't I?"

Brady snorted. "Get up. Get into teams. We're gonna play some ball, and then we're gonna get pissed."

Everyone was staring at Brady.

"What?" he growled.

"Dude," Aidan said. "You just spoke in several whole sentences, like, in a row."

Brady glowered at us. "Ball. Now."

The guys got up and pulled me up with them. Aidan slung an arm around my shoulders as we headed out of the lounge.

I didn't know what tomorrow would bring, I didn't know what tests the fortress and the knights would put us through, or if I'd make it through the break to next term. But I knew one thing. Whatever I did, these guys would have my back, and right now.

Right now, I was going to play ball and get drunk.

To be continued...
Indigo's journey continues in *Shadow Weaver* book 2 in
The Nightwatch Academy Series Grab it here:
https://www.amazon.com/dp/B07VK9WYI9

OTHER BOOKS BY DEBBIE CASSIDY

The Gatekeeper Chronicles

Coauthored with Jasmine Walt

Marked by Sin

Hunted by Sin

Claimed by Sin

The Witch Blood Chronicles

(Spin-off to the Gatekeeper Chronicles)

Binding Magick

Defying Magick

Embracing Magick

Unleashing Magick

The Fearless Destiny Series

Beyond Everlight

Into Evernight

Under Twilight

The Chronicles of Midnight

Protector of Midnight

Champion of Midnight

Secrets of Midnight

Shades of Midnight

Savior of Midnight

Chronicles of Arcana

City of Demons

City of the Lost

City of Everdark

City of War

For the Blood

For the Blood

For the Power

For the Reign

For the Hunt (novella)

Heart of Darkness

Captive of Darkness

Bane of Winter

Fate's Destiny

Deadworld

Deadworld

Dead City

Dead Sea

Dead End

The Nightwatch Academy

Shadow Caster

Shadow Weaver

Survivor's Heart (Planet Athion World)

Novella series

Rogue

Rebel

Survivor

Standalone Novellas

Blood Blade

ABOUT THE AUTHOR

Debbie Cassidy lives in England, Bedfordshire, with her three kids and very supportive husband. Coffee and chocolate biscuits are her writing fuels of choice, and she is still working on getting that perfect tower of solitude built in her back garden. Obsessed with building new worlds and reading about them, she spends her spare time daydreaming and conversing with the characters in her head – in a totally non psychotic way of course. She writes High Fantasy, Urban Fantasy, Space Fantasy, and Reverse Harem. Connect with Debbie via her website at debbiecassidyauthor.com or twitter @authordcassidy. Or sign up to her Newsletter to stay in the know.

Made in the USA
San Bernardino, CA
16 December 2019

61690998R00202